"Willie,

His words made her look at him suspiciously. Why did the idea of a deal with this man suddenly make Willie feel as if she'd just agreed to strike a bargain with the devil?

"What kind of a deal?" she inquired cautiously, and he laughed at the distrustful expression on her face.

"Nothing as ominous as you're thinking. Here's the deal: I'll help you find T.C. if you promise to reconsider my application to have the boy come and live with me."

"That's blackmail!" she cried, appalled. "Besides," she added, "it's your *job* to find T.C."

"And it's *your* job to find a good home for him. I can provide it for him, Willie. Just because we don't see eye to eye on things doesn't mean you shouldn't at least give me a fair chance. What do you say?"

Somewhat hesitantly, Willie spoke. "It's a deal, Ryce."

Dear Reader:

The spirit of the Silhouette Romance Homecoming Celebration lives on as each month we bring you six books by continuing stars!

And we have a galaxy of stars planned for 1988. In the coming months, we're publishing romances by many of your favorite authors such as Annette Broadrick, Sondra Stanford and Brittany Young. And that's not all—during the summer, Diana Palmer presents her most engaging heroes and heroines in a trilogy that will be sure to capture your heart!

Your response to these authors and other authors of Silhouette Romances has served as a touchstone for us, and we're pleased to bring you more books with Silhouette's distinctive medley of charm, wit and—above all—romance.

I hope you enjoy this book and the many stories to come. Come home to romance—for always!

Sincerely,

Tara Hughes
Senior Editor
Silhouette Books

SHARON DE VITA

Sherlock's Home

Silhouette Romance

Published by Silhouette Books New York

America's Publisher of Contemporary Romance

This book is dedicated to three very special children:
my own

To Jeanne, Annie and Tony, you guys have given me
the best (and a few of the worst) moments of my life. I
hope I have given you the confidence to believe in
yourself, and the magic of your dreams.
Love, Mom

SILHOUETTE BOOKS
300 E. 42nd St., New York, N.Y. 10017

ISBN: 0-373-08593-1

First Silhouette Books printing August 1988

Printed in the U.S.A.

Books by Sharon DeVita

Silhouette Romance

Heavenly Match #475
Lady and the Legend #498
Kane and Mabel #545
Baby Makes Three #573
Sherlock's Home #593

SHARON DE VITA

decided around her thirtieth birthday that she wanted to produce something that didn't have to be walked or fed during the night. An eternal optimist who always believes in happy endings, she felt romances were the perfect vehicles for her creative energies. As a reader, and a writer, she prefers stories that are fun and light-hearted, and tries to inject these qualities in her own work. This mother of three is happily married to her high school sweetheart.

The author gratefully acknowledges
and appreciates the help of:

Ms. Jody Lowenthal, Attorney at Law

AND

Mr. Richard Brzeczek, Attorney at Law

Chapter One

Clutching a battered file folder in her hand, Wilhelmina Walker marched staunchly down the precinct hallway. Her temper increased with every click of her heels on the worn linoleum floor. She should have known better than to trust a man whose biceps were bigger than his brains!

For the past three weeks, ever since she'd taken over as head of the Children's Welfare Agency, Detective Michael Ryce had been a thorn in her slender side.

Ryce was a juvenile detective, *juvenile* being the key word, Wilhelmina thought sourly, and their paths—not to mention their swords—had crossed often during the past few weeks.

Mutinous in the face of authority, Ryce was brash, brazen and pugnacious. And those were his good points!

Up until now Wilhelmina had allowed him some leeway, certain that once he became more familiar with the way she operated, they could come to some sort of...understanding. But now the man had gone too far; he'd pushed her too far.

Ryce may have been allowed to con or sidestep around her predecessor, but he wasn't going to be allowed such liberties while she was in charge!

As head of the agency, it was *her* job to assess and approve foster homes for the children in her care. Not his. He had no right to interfere in the care and custody of the children in her ward. While she was in charge, she fully intended to see to it that Ryce follow the rules to the letter. And that included keeping his meddling, interfering hands out of her business! And she fully intended to tell him so.

Pausing outside Ryce's door, Wilhelmina took a deep breath and smoothed back an errant lock of ebony hair. She would remain calm and professional, detached and impersonal. She would not allow the man to goad her into losing her temper. Again.

Impartial and impersonal, she cautioned herself as she threw open his door and marched inside. With her posture erect, her carriage precise, Wilhelmina stalked across the room, coming to a halt directly in front of the cluttered mess he called a desk.

Ryce was slouched low in his chair; his booted feet were propped atop his desk, and his nose was buried behind the afternoon newspaper. He didn't even have the courtesy to look up to acknowledge her presence. Wilhelmina's resolve to hang on to her temper flew out the window.

"Are you out of your mind?" she demanded. *So much for remaining cool and detached,* she thought dismally, annoyed that the man's mere insolent presence could provoke her.

"The other day you said I didn't *have* a mind, re-member?" Ryce countered, without bothering to look at her.

She took a step closer. "Just what do you think you're doing?" she inquired, waving T. C. Sherlock's battered file folder in his direction.

"I'm trying to read the paper," he grumbled, turning another page and doing his best to ignore her. From the tone of her voice, Ryce had a feeling she'd already made up her mind about him. So what the hell was the point, he wondered, casually flipping another page.

Wilhelmina took a deep breath, spacing her words carefully. "Detective Ryce, you had no right to prom-ise T. C. Sherlock that *you* would be his new foster parent." The thought brought on a shudder. Putting a homeless eleven-year-old child in Ryce's care would be like putting the inmates in charge of the asylum! Ryce was more suited to raising hell than to raising a child.

"Something wrong with me, Willie?" he inquired, using an abbreviation of her name in order to annoy her. He continued reading, deliberately trying to ag-gravate her. Why not? It was clear she'd made her de-cision. Long ago he'd learned to never let anyone know what you were thinking. Or feeling. If they didn't know, they couldn't hurt you. And she would never know how much T.C. meant to him. He had his pride, and he would rather choke on it than swallow it.

"Detective Ryce? Detective Ryce!" Wilhelmina yanked down one corner of the newspaper so that he would be forced to look at her. "How many times have you been suspended from the force?"

"This year?" he inquired, reaching up to absently scratch his brow. His eyes, big, bold and enormously blue, slowly lifted to hers. His gaze, glinting with a hint of amusement, pinned hers, and Wilhelmina took a deep breath. *Those eyes,* she thought dully, feeling her pulse respond to him despite herself, *ought to be outlawed.*

Wilhelmina took a deep breath, struggling to gather her scattered composure. "What did you make for dinner last night?"

"Reservations," he growled.

"How many... relationships have you had during the past year?" She shifted uncomfortably.

"How much time do we have?" he asked, dropping the newspaper into a heap and making a great show of looking at his watch before grinning into her belligerent face.

"Detective Ryce." Her voice was tight with control. "You know very well as head of the Children's Welfare Agency it's *my* job to assess, choose and approve foster homes. Not *yours.* I simply cannot and will not tolerate any more of your interference."

One dark brow lifted, and his eyes darkened, but Wilhelmina was not about to be deterred. "You had no right to discuss this matter with T.C. before you discussed it with me. I have a legal, moral and ethical responsibility to protect the children." Now that she had his full attention, she took a cautious step closer. The man had to be made aware of all the implications of his actions.

"Detective Ryce, I will not allow you to give T.C. any more false hope of empty promises. That child has been through enough. He's been booted around from foster home to foster home, he's—"

"Willie," he barked, lowering his feet to the floor with a thud. The sound echoed as loudly as a cannon in the quiet room, and she jumped. Why did the man have the ability to make her as nervous as a scalded cat, she wondered darkly, annoyed at herself as well as him.

"I think you'd better start looking in your own backyard," he suggested, his tone of voice causing her protests to evaporate. "You want to talk about false hope and empty promises? You and that damn agency of yours are the ones who've been finding those so-called 'homes' for T.C. You find him a home; he runs away. Then you call me, I find the kid, turn him back over to you, and the cycle starts all over again. You know the old saying," Ryce added, lifting his cold steely gaze to hers, "People who live in glass houses shouldn't throw stones."

Anger ripped through her. How dare he criticize her! She did the best she could with what she had to work with, and his meddling and interference certainly weren't helping matters.

"Perhaps if *you* wouldn't interfere in my job," she snapped, glaring down her nose at him, "I wouldn't have such a hard time doing it. And I really don't think it's of your concern how I handle the children or conduct the affairs of the agency!"

"Affairs?" Ryce drew the word out brazenly, causing a heated flush to suffuse her cheeks. "An unmarried lady like yourself? Why, Ms. Walker, I'm shocked. Here I thought we were talking about T.C., but apparently we're talking about something else altogether." Leaning back in his chair, Ryce laced his hands behind his head and allowed his gaze to do a thorough search and sweep of her. He intimately in-

vestigated everything from the top of her silky black hair caught somberly behind her head, to the tips of her low-heeled, sensible shoes—pausing long enough to thoroughly examine everything in between. Twice.

The intensity of his gaze held her spellbound as shivers of heat soared through her, touching her in a way that both frightened and fascinated her. Despite his faults there was something about Ryce, something wildly, wickedly attractive. And he knew it.

His visual investigation ended, and he brought his gaze back to rest on her mouth, which was puckered in open annoyance. "So tell me, Willie," he growled, lowering his voice to a husky whisper. "How do you conduct your... *affairs*? By the book, no doubt," he concluded with a lazy grin that caused her pulse to scamper wildly. "Everything by the book, right, Willie? Oh, and let's not forget the rules."

Twin blotches of color scorched her cheeks. If Ryce thought those seductive looks he was giving her were having any effect, he was wrong, she thought darkly. Dead wrong.

Well, she amended, acknowledging the increased tempo of her pulse, they were *hardly* having any effect on her.

"Ryce," she snapped, ignoring his crass innuendos and trying to channel her thoughts back to the problem at hand, "you know as well as I do that in order to even be *considered* as a foster parent, a person must be responsible and reliable. Someone who knows the rules and adheres to them." Wilhelmina drew herself up, inhaling a great gust of air through her nose. "It is my professional opinion that *you* wouldn't know how to adhere to a rule if they rolled you in glue!" The sharpness of her words reverberated through the quiet room. Blast! She'd let the man get to her again. No one had ever had the power to raise her tongue or her temper the way this man did!

Long, silent moments plodded by as she tried to harness her emotions. What was it about the man, she wondered crossly, that caused her usually practical, sensible emotions to go askew? She'd dealt with all kinds of people over the years, rude people, ill-mannered people and even some unclean people. But no one had the power to raise her temper or her pulse the way this man did.

Maybe it was his size. Lord knows, the man was big enough to scare the stripes off a tiger. And that voice of his was low and deep, with a husky quality that set her nerves rattling. But no, Wilhelmina knew it was more than that.

It had more to do with the way he carried and conducted himself. Ryce was hard, cold and tough, exactly what an inner-city cop should be. But he was more than that. He was also rude, rough and rawboned, with a tumble of pitch-black curls that fell recklessly around a face that was blatant in it's attractiveness. His features were dwarfed by his eyes—so big, blue and bold, they always seemed to be mocking the world and everyone in it. His full, cocky mouth always seemed poised on the brink of a devilish smile. As if he knew something the rest of the world didn't.

Like now.

"Don't think you're going to charm or con your way around me," Wilhelmina threatened crossly. "In addition to being responsible and reliable, you know very well there are certain rules and regulations that foster parents must abide, not to mention the procedures that have to be adhered to—"

"Willie," Ryce barked, startling her to attention. "I suggest you take your rules and your regulations and ... um ... don't forget your procedures, and stick them in your—" he looked up at her and grinned rakishly "—file."

Her mouth fell open in stunned disbelief. "How dare you!" she cried, slamming T.C.'s file down on his desk and sending a pile of debris sailing to the floor. "How dare you speak to me in such a—"

"Why, Ms. Walker!" Ryce drew back and looked up at her in genuine surprise. "My ... my ... my ..." Clucking his tongue in admonition, Ryce dropped his hands over hers and gave her a patronizing little pat. His fingers were warm, sending a heated wave of awareness rolling over her. "I never knew you had such a temper. Why, honey, you're so mad, you're liable to pop the buttons on that starched little blouse of yours." His eyes boldly lowered to the front of her blouse. Slowly they coasted, lingering on each and every button until Wilhelmina's heart thumped about like a fish out of water. The man was insufferable!

"I am not mad," she lied, trying to snatch her hands from his and almost falling off her low-heeled shoes in her effort to free herself. "I don't have a temper and I am *not* your honey!" she cried, finally wrenching her hands free of his and almost tumbling backward in her mad scramble to freedom.

"Yes, I can see that you don't have a temper," Ryce agreed, nodding his head. "You're not mad, either," he assured her, letting a crooked little smile break loose.

Wilhelmina inhaled gustily, trying to bank down the rage bubbling inside. "Just because you have a badge and a gun, you think you're immune from the rules," she snapped coldly. "You think you know all the answers, don't you? Let me tell you something—"

"Honey," Ryce said, laughing softly. "By the time *I* figured out all the answers, someone had changed the questions."

Wilhelmina drew back. "I'm in no mood for this," she warned, trying to ignore the insolent smile on his lips.

"Well, Willie, what are you in the mood for? Personally, I could go for some pastrami, but whatever you want is fine with me." Ryce leaned back farther in his chair and angled his head to get a better look at her legs. "I'm easy," he murmured huskily, his tone clearly indicating that his morals were no doubt as loose as his tongue. "Whatever you want is fine with me." His eyes met hers in open masculine appreciation, and Wilhelmina pursed her lips. What she wanted at this moment could probably get her ten years to life just for thinking about it!

"Ryce," she said indignantly, drawing his name out and deliberately making him sound like something that had just slithered out of a drainpipe, "I have spent too many years dealing with government bureaucrats, unmanageable children and cranky foster parents to let the whims of one cantankerous, contrary cop poised on the cusp of craziness throw me off stride!"

"Willie!" He drew back and did his best to look offended. "Now if I didn't know better, I'd think you just insulted me."

Insulted him! Wilhelmina squared her shoulders. "I'm warning you, I won't tolerate any more of your interference. I will not allow you to lead T.C. on and perhaps give him more heartbreak. Do you hear me?"

Ryce wasn't listening. He was absently staring at the untamed riot of ebony curls that had slipped free of the coil she'd nailed to the back of her head. Why the hell does she wear her hair all scraped back like that? he wondered. It was a glorious blue-black color and looked as soft as silk, but all bound up like that, she resembled a skinned chicken. She was much too young to wear those neat, efficient clothes, too, he decided, letting his eyes wander over her again. She favored those dark skirts and pristine little white blouses. Her legs—what he could see with those dowdy little skirts of hers—were gorgeous, incredibly long and sexy.

Wilhelmina Walker wasn't a beauty, that was for sure. But she was attractive, too damn attractive for his peace of mind. He didn't like the way he found himself thinking about her or visualizing her. With the determined set of her chin, the straight arch of her back and the flames shooting out of those gray eyes of hers, he found himself intrigued by a woman for the first time in a long, long while. It was a feeling he wasn't comfortable with. With her dander up, Wilhelmina Walker was a sight to behold. She was like a flash of sunlight in his dark life. Bright, warm and glowing. When you saw only darkness, sometimes it was difficult to recognize the light.

Ryce sighed heavily, lost in thought. Fifteen years as a cop had taken it's toll. His job had made him distrustful of everyone. People, the system and even the stinking rules that made no sense or difference anyway.

But Willie was young and eager and so full of fire-and-brimstone determination, he had to admire her. She was so damn sure she could make a difference.

He'd been like her once upon a time, he thought, before frustration and complacency had set in. He knew when the day of reckoning finally came, when Willie realized no matter what she did, she couldn't make one bit of difference, she was going to get burned. And burned bad. Ryce felt a growing bond of protectiveness for her. And he didn't like it, not at all.

Hell, he'd been trying for fifteen years to make a difference, and he had finally come to terms with the fact that the rules and regulations coupled with the limitations and frustrations of his job prevented him from barely making a dent. They just had too much responsibility and too little power. The rules were the rules, and the system was the system, and there was nothing anyone could do to change it. Not even Willie Walker.

Now he was just putting in his time.

Doing time, his mind corrected, and Ryce swore softly. He was doing time just as surely as the criminals he'd put away over the years. Maybe that's why T.C. meant so much to him. The kid was his chance to make a difference.

Part of Ryce's life and all of his heart had been closed off to everyone a long, long time ago. He'd learned to gather his emotions and hoard them in a tiny little space inside of him that he allowed no one to touch.

Until he met T.C.

The kid had somehow managed to wiggle his way into that little space. Maybe it was because Ryce recognized something of himself in T.C. There was a hopelessness about the kid, a ragged fear about the homeless waif, that tore at Ryce's heart.

Muttering an oath, Ryce dragged a hand through his hair and banished his own miserable, youthful memories. He was too old for these trips down memory lane, he thought in disgust, knowing that no matter what, the memories still haunted him.

Aware that Ryce was looking at her but not paying the least bit of attention to what she was saying, Wilhelmina rapped her knuckles on the top of his desk in an effort to get his attention. "Detective Ryce?"

His gaze flew to hers. "Oh, hell," he muttered in disgust, suddenly feeling old and sad and just a bit empty, and knowing she was responsible. He *must* be getting soft, letting a woman and a kid get to him.

"Detective Ryce!" Wilhelmina repeated. This man was going to try her patience to the limits. And then some.

"Willie, don't you have someone else to annoy?" Ryce growled, laying his head back on his chair. Trying to ignore the feelings that were taunting him, and put some distance between himself and this woman, Ryce closed his eyes, effectively dismissing her. He didn't like the way he responded to her. He didn't like the feelings she aroused in him. He had to keep her at bay, keep a safe distance between them. Complications like her he didn't need in his life, not now, not ever. "Willie, surely a busybody do-gooder like yourself could find someone else to bother. I think I've had my fair share for one day."

Wilhelmina stiffened. "I don't have to take this abuse from you," she said indignantly.

"Yeah, I know," he admitted, trying to banish a grin. "There are people standing in line just waiting to abuse you poor, overworked social workers. Right, Willie?" Ryce lifted his head. Opening his eyes, he let his gaze drop to her lips, parted now with the effort of breathing. Her mouth looked so soft, so...inviting. What would it feel like to have her lips beneath his? Pushing the thought away, he dropped his gaze to the top of his desk and absently picked up T.C.'s folder, determined not to let her get to him.

Wilhelmina snatched the file from his hands, clutching it closely to her chest, as if to protect T.C. from him. "Detective Ryce, I am hereby putting you on formal notice. If you continue to disobey and disregard the rules as far as they concern me and the children in my care—specifically T.C.—I will personally go to your superiors, lodge a formal complaint and then see to it that you are tossed off the force on your arrogant, insufferable rear end. Do you hear me?" Her words echoed around the room, and Ryce's gaze flew to hers. Unconsciously, Wilhelmina stepped back as his bold blue eyes collided with hers in open challenge.

"That sounds like a threat," Ryce murmured, and Wilhelmina froze. She was no dummy. She recognized the sound of danger when she heard it.

"It's not a...threat," she stammered. "It's...a...promise."

His hands hit the desk, and he rolled to his feet in one quick, graceful motion. Wilhelmina's breath caught in her throat. Clutching the file folder tighter to her chest, she took a step backward.

Why on earth hadn't she listened to her mother, she wondered wildly. Hadn't her mother always told her to wear clean underwear, sit like a lady and *never* argue with someone wearing a gun? Wilhelmina eyed the menacing-looking weapon strapped under Ryce's arm. Well, she thought glumly, two out of three aren't bad.

Ryce sauntered leisurely around the desk, coming to a stop directly in front of her. She gazed up at him cautiously. Feeling trapped, she slowly began to inch back and away from him until her hips were pressed against his desk.

"Willie," Ryce sighed her name and took a step closer. His sweet breath glanced off her face in soft drifts. She could feel the warmth of his body, smell his faintly musky cologne. Her thoughts stalled. Ryce smelled of . . . danger. Somehow it was heady and just a bit exciting. Her knees grew weak, and her breath whistled through her trembling lips.

Lifting his hand, Ryce gently ran his finger down the soft curve of her cheek, tenderly pushing aside a loose tendril of hair. Her skin seemed to come alive under his touch, and her eyes hesitantly met his.

She was suddenly and vividly aware of his masculinity. She was reacting to him like a . . . woman, and not at all like a professional. Still, the woman in her couldn't help but notice the way a lock of his hair fell across his forehead. The way his eyes changed from light to dark. The way his massive chest moved with each and every breath. Wilhelmina glanced up at him again, her gaze drawn to his as she struggled to find and maintain a professional air.

Ryce slid his finger to her chin, tilting her head back until she was forced to look at him. She swallowed convulsively as her heart began to thud wildly. She glanced away, wanting to look at anything—everything—but him.

"Willie," he growled softly, leaning close and holding her startled gaze until her knees threatened to buckle. "You are the most high-strung, stiff-lipped, rigid pain in the—" he grinned rakishly, and lightly fingered the collar of her blouse "—backside I have ever met."

Wilhelmina peeled her collar out of his hand. She opened her mouth to issue an angry retort, but the words slid back down her throat as Ryce placed a gentle finger to her lips. Her skin burned from his touch, and she made a conscious effort to ignore her response to him.

"Now," he continued quietly, holding her gaze until her nerves began to thrum like distant thunder. "I've got a trick knee, indigestion and a bad temper. I have put up with your lectures, your rules and even your damn regulations. And," he added with a lift of his brow, "I've also put up with your rather verbal opinions of me. But, honey, I've never made a promise I didn't keep. Not to T.C. or to anyone else. And I don't take kindly to threats. Official or otherwise."

"Neither do I," she returned shakily, looking up at him in disbelief. Where was the charming quipster, she wondered, surprised by the seriousness of the man looming over her. Obviously there was something more to Ryce than a charming smile and a cavalier attitude.

She had a responsibility to protect the children. Why couldn't she make him understand that? Didn't Ryce know that by sidestepping and conning his way around the rules that he was only hurting himself and, perhaps, T.C. And she couldn't—no, she wouldn't—allow it.

A sudden thought occurred to her. "Ryce, why do you want to take T.C. in, anyway?" She watched a flash of hope flicker then die in his big blue eyes.

"What difference does it make? You've already told me I'm not suitable, right, Willie?" He didn't wait for her to answer. "I'm not responsible, either? Did it ever occur to you that T.C. might need me?" He continued to hold her gaze until her heart thudded wickedly beneath her breast.

"N-no," she stammered truthfully. The thought had never occurred to her. T.C. needed a lot of things, but she wasn't certain he needed a rebellious cop who wouldn't know a rule or responsibility if it walked up and bit him on his arrogant rear end.

Or did he?

The idea stunned her. Perhaps she'd been too quick to judge Ryce. Perhaps she *had* let her personal feelings and opinions of the man interfere with her professional assessment of the situation.

She opened her mouth to say something, but Ryce leaned close until nothing but his face filled her vision. He was so close, his breath ruffled the few curls that had slipped loose. Her thudding heart echoed in her ears, and T.C.'s folder slipped through her nerveless fingers, sending the contents sailing to the floor. On shaky legs, Wilhelmina bent down to retrieve the fallen items, grateful for a few moments to compose herself.

"Willie?"

"What!" Lowering her head, Wilhelmina tried to ignore the man and put all her concentration into the task at hand. It was difficult with him so close.

"Oh, hell," Ryce growled, bending down next to her until the heat of his body washed over her. "Let me help you." He reached out, but Wilhelmina pushed his hand away.

"I don't need your help," she replied stiffly, gathering her papers in her arms. It was difficult to think clearly with him so close.

Ryce frowned at the distressed look on her face. Maybe he'd pushed her too far. He'd been rough on her, but, damn, what the hell did she expect? She had come tearing into his office, throwing insults and accusations at him, telling him he wasn't suitable for T.C. How else did she expect him to act?

"Willie," he said gently, feeling a twinge of guilt. "Are you all right?" His voice was so soft, so earnest, Wilhelmina glanced up at him in surprise. His gaze caught and held hers. Blinking rapidly, she swallowed hard. His mouth was only inches from hers. *So close,* she thought hazily. The papers slid from her fingers again.

Heaving an exasperated sigh, Ryce reached out, scooped her papers up with one hand, then clamped his fingers around her elbow with the other. In one quick motion, he rose, pulling Wilhelmina up with him.

She looked at him.

He looked at her.

Wilhelmina's chest rose, stopping in midbreath. His fingers were still wrapped around her elbow, gently stroking her, coaxing a response. His touch seared through the fabric of her blouse, engulfing her in a rush of heat. Her lips parted with a soft feminine sigh. He was so close. His eyes, she thought absently, were...beautiful...sad. Why, she wondered?

His gaze settled on her mouth. So...soft. So...tempting. So...inviting. The urge to protect her grew stronger, and unconsciously his fingers tightened. He could feel the tremors shake her as the heat of his body seeped into hers.

"Ryce?" She whispered his name as a thousand unnamed emotions overcame her.

Something forbidden wiggled into that tiny spot inside of him. Instinctively Ryce drew back, refusing to face the emotions storming him. He unwound his fingers from her arm, and the contact was broken. They both took a step backward.

Damn! He was getting soft for sure. With an oath of disgust, Ryce pressed her fallen items into her trembling hands. He couldn't—no, he wouldn't—let her get to him. She was getting too close. He was feeling things he shouldn't feel. Wilhelmina Walker, with her wide-eyed innocence and her fire-and-brimstone determination, was touching him in ways that— His thoughts broke off. He had to put some distance between them. Now.

"You know, Willie, you've got to learn not to take this job so seriously." Ryce grinned mischievously, wanting only to break the oppressive mood that seemed to be drawing him closer to her. "It's not good for your health. Why, you just might get an ulcer." He looked decidedly pleased at the prospect, and Wilhelmina stared at him. A moment ago she'd wondered where the cocky, cavalier Ryce was; now she wished she could send him back to wherever it was he'd gone!

"I don't believe my health is any of your concern," she snapped, knowing full well that the only thing liable to give her an ulcer was him! "It's not enough that you have to meddle in my job, now you want to meddle in my life? Is there no end to your audacity?"

"I don't know why you're so riled," he said cheerfully, as she pushed past him and headed for the door. "I was only trying to help."

"I don't believe I asked for, nor do I need, your help," she called, not bothering to slow her pace any.

She'd had enough of this man for one day. Perhaps for one lifetime.

"Willie, you've hurt me," he teased, not looking in the least bit offended. "I'll have you know that I'm generally thought to be a very helpful person."

Helpful! Wilhelmina shuddered. At the moment she could think of quite a few things to call Ryce, but "helpful" surely wasn't one of them.

"Detective Ryce," she hissed coldly, coming to a halt and swiveling her head in his direction. "I can assure you that ducks will wear diapers long before *I* ever ask for your help!" She lunged for the door, yanking it open with such force it jammed against her toe and bounced closed again. "And don't call me Willie!" she cried, hating the offensive nickname.

"You're right, Willie doesn't really suit you. *Meany* suits you much better." His soft laughter filled the room, and she glared at him. "Does this mean I'm not going to get T.C.?" Ryce inquired sweetly, and Wilhelmina whirled on him.

Lifting her chin, she leveled him with a gaze that should have frozen him to the spot. "Detective Ryce," she said slowly, enunciating her words as if she were speaking to a thickheaded child, "I'm personally going to see to it that you get *exactly* what you deserve!"

Chapter Two

Someone ought to lock that man up!" Favoring her stubbed toe, Wilhelmina limped past her all-too-interested assistant and slammed into her office, muttering imprecations about Ryce's birthright and behavior.

"More problems with the detective?" Fergie inquired with a knowing look, as she planted herself firmly in the doorway of Wilhelmina's office.

"Problems?" Wilhelmina cried, dropping T.C.'s folder on to her immaculate desk and flopping into her chair. The animosity between her and Detective Ryce was no secret.

"Had another run-in, did you?" Fergie inquired, trying to conceal a grin.

Shaking her head, Wilhelmina slid her shoe off to rub her toe. "The man's—" She glanced up at Fergie and blushed. What the man was couldn't be repeated. At least not out loud. "The man's . . . impossible."

"Impossible?" Fergie sighed, a dreamy smile on her face. "Honey, he may be impossible, but darn good-looking." Fergie wiggled her brows suggestively. "Ryce can read me *my* rights anytime."

Wilhelmina glared at her. She was in no mood to hear about Ryce's charms. She was well aware of them, more aware than she should be.

"Why on earth would Ryce want to take a foster child into his home, anyway?" Wilhelmina grumbled. "If the man even has a home. Judging from the condition of his office, I wouldn't be surprised to learn the man lives in a dirt-floored hovel somewhere underground."

"A dirt-floored hovel you say?" Fergie repeated, rocking back on her heels and watching her boss with interest.

"And even if I did have a temporary lapse in sanity," Wilhelmina went on, "and wanted to consider Ryce as a foster parent, he had no business talking to T.C. about it until he talked to me!" T.C. had been through enough, and she wasn't quite certain how much more the poor child could bear. Five foster homes in two years, and the kid had run away from every one of them. At the moment, she had T.C. living in an emergency shelter, but she had every indication he was getting ready to bolt again. The thought saddened her and made her all the more determined to find just the right, suitable home for him. *Suitable* was the key word. That definitely left Ryce out. T.C. needed a secure, safe environment, where he could get the love, attention and devotion he needed in order to thrive and prosper. What he didn't need was an obstinate, rebellious, undisciplined cop who walked a tightrope between insanity and instability.

Wilhelmina's scowl deepened as she raised her eyes
to her assistant. She tried to banish all thoughts of the
meddlesome detective. "What's going on here?"

"Got a few leads on a home for T.C.," Fergie said
abruptly, sensing her boss's displeasure. "Left them
on your desk."

Wilhelmina nodded and picked up the sheets off her
desk. "I'll get to work on these right now. We've got
to find a permanent home for him, Fergie. One he
won't run away from. This morning I had to tell T.C.
that he wouldn't be going to live with Detective Ryce."
The burden of her responsibilities weighed heavily on
her mind, and Wilhelmina's shoulders slumped.

"How'd it go?" Fergie inquired, her face drawn
into a frown.

Wilhelmina sighed sadly, rubbing her toe more vig-
orously. "About as well as could be expected. It was
probably one of the hardest things I've had to do. But,
Fergie, you know as well as I do that Ryce is hardly
parent material. The man can barely take care of
himself, let alone a child." Wilhelmina's gaze drifted
off into the distance as she painfully remembered her
conversation with the boy. "T.C. was so upset. I tried
to explain it to him so that he could understand. I assured him that we're working on the problem and that
we'd find him a permanent home. Soon." Still, the
child was obviously upset, and it was all Ryce's fault,
she thought darkly. If he hadn't made promises he
couldn't keep and had no right making, she wouldn't
be in this fix. *Poor T.C.,* she thought sadly. This was
all Ryce's fault. And he had the nerve to call *her* a
busybody!

Of course, T.C. couldn't understand why Ryce was
totally unsuitable as a foster parent. She wasn't about

to place T.C. in Ryce's care only to have him grow tired of the responsibility and then decide parenthood wasn't for him. She couldn't afford that, but more importantly, neither could T.C.

"Don't worry, boss," Fergie assured her. "Something will come up. It always does. There goes the other line. Want some coffee?" Fergie narrowed her gaze. "And I think I better grab an ice pack for that toe while I'm at it." Fergie paused for a moment. "You wouldn't want to tell me how you got that sore toe, would you?" Fergie asked, her eyes twinkling wickedly.

"I would not," Wilhelmina confirmed. She would die before she admitted to Fergie or to anyone else that she'd totally lost her cool, not to mention her temper, and rammed her own foot with a door. She was embarrassed that she'd let Ryce get to her. She had a feeling the man had deliberately tried to aggravate her. And, she thought glumly, he'd succeeded. But why, she wondered.

Why did he take such great pleasure in trying to drive her crazy with his unorthodox methods of dealing with kids—*her* kids. He'd done some irregular things in the three weeks since she'd taken over, but his latest escapade with T.C. was blatant, even for Ryce. Wilhelmina sighed.

The first time T.C. had run away, she'd notified the Chicago police, and they in turn began their search. As luck would have it, Detective Ryce was the officer who found T.C.; and instead of contacting her immediately or turning the child over to an emergency shelter as the rules dictated, Ryce had ignored proper procedure and taken T.C. home with him.

The child had taken an instant shine to the man, although Wilhelmina had no idea why. Probably because Ryce had an eleven-year-old's mentality, she thought darkly. From what she had gathered from the child, they'd played cards, eaten carryouts and talked long into the night. By the time Ryce had finally turned T.C. over to her, almost twenty-four hours later, T.C. was determined not to go back to the foster home. He wanted to stay with Ryce. Wilhelmina had to admit there seemed to be a genuine affection between the man and the boy, but that just wasn't enough. Raising a child was entirely different from spending one night with him. She had the child's long-term future to think of.

The idea of placing T.C. in Ryce's care was totally out of the question as far as she was concerned. She'd only been on the job a week the first time T.C. had run away, and in that week, she'd gotten very well acquainted with Ryce's unorthodox methods. Despite the way he operated, doing things his own way and on his own time, he *was* good with children. Very good. She had to give him that. But he was just so...unorthodox, so unreliable, so unsettled. She had no idea what brazen thing the man would do next. She couldn't put T.C. in Ryce's custody when she wasn't absolutely certain he was the best person for the child. She couldn't afford to make a mistake and, more importantly, T.C. couldn't afford it.

Ryce had no business taking T.C. home with him in the first place, she thought sourly. Or in promising the child that he would try to get custody of him. The idea was absurd. Absolutely absurd. And now, because of his unorthodox behavior, she was the one who had had to tell T.C. he couldn't go to live with Ryce. Remembering the child's disappointment, her anger at the man grew all over again. Her fingers itched to throttle Detective Ryce. Instead, heaving an exasperated sigh, she picked up her telephone.

Two hours later, Wilhelmina patiently dialed the final number on the list Fergie had given her. So far she'd drawn a big, fat zero. She had absolutely no luck in finding a permanent home for T.C. While she knew children of his age were hard to place, it looked like this task was going to be darn near impossible. She had to find a home for him, she thought firmly, she simply had to!

"Yes, I know how difficult an eleven-year-old can be," she said, shifting the phone from one ear to the other as she spoke to the person on the other end—a mother who already had six foster children, plus two of her own. "But surely—"

"Boss, I have to talk to you. Now!" Fergie, hands on hips, was firmly planted in Wilhelmina's doorway again. Wilhelmina's eyes slid closed, and she tried to concentrate on her own conversation and ignore her assistant, but the formidable Fergie was hard to ignore. Perhaps that's why she was so good at her job. Wilhelmina knew that Fergie wasn't about to give up until she'd had her say. Or her way. Whichever came first.

Wilhelmina waved Fergie away as the woman on the other end of the receiver politely but firmly listed all the reasons why she and her husband simply couldn't accept another child.

"Boss! We've got another crisis on line two!" With bulldog determination, Fergie high-stepped it across Wilhelmina's office, planting herself firmly in front of her desk. "It's T.C.," Fergie said urgently, and Wilhelmina's gaze flew to her assistant's. Blindly, Wilhelmina hung up the phone, feeling a dawning sense of foreboding engulf her.

"T.C.?" she repeated weakly.

"He's gone," Fergie said simply.

"Gone?" Wilhelmina inquired blankly, as her mind struggled to assemble all the information. "Gone where?"

"Now if I knew that," Fergie retorted, planting her hands on her ample hips and scowling, "would I be in here bothering you?"

Wilhelmina ran a weary hand across her eyes as if to forestall the problem at hand. "How long has he been gone?"

"As far as I can tell, since this morning. He left for school as usual, and he never came home. Didn't go to school, either. I checked." Fergie cocked her head. "Should I call Ryce?"

"Ryce!" The name hissed out of Wilhelmina's mouth. Now why did she have a feeling T.C.'s latest disappearance just might be something Ryce would know about? "Don't bother," Wilhelmina ordered, picking up the phone and quickly dialing Ryce's office. "I'll do it myself. If I find out that man had anything to do with— Yes, hello. This is Wilhelmina Walker, from the Children's Welfare Agency. I'd like to talk to Detective Ryce." Her eyes widened, and she gave Fergie a knowing look. "Gone for the weekend, you say. May I have his address, please. It's urgent that I contact him." Grabbing a pencil, Wilhelmina quickly jotted down Ryce's address, said a hurried goodbye and grabbed her jacket off the back of her chair.

"Boss," Fergie said worriedly, "where are you going?"

"To get T.C.," Wilhelmina replied, grabbing Ryce's address off her desk and stuffing her sore foot back into her shoe. "After I throttle one arrogant, insufferable cop!"

With dastardly deeds working their way through her mind, Wilhelmina jerked her car to a halt in front of Ryce's house and limped up the driveway. When she got her hands on Ryce she was going to...well, she was certain she would think up something suitable, something to fit the occasion. Like lynching!

How dare he? she seethed. Who the hell did he think he was? What absolute, unmitigated nerve, she thought, yanking open the screen door and jamming her finger against his doorbell. She'd warned him, but apparently the man hadn't paid any attention to their conversation this afternoon .

She had no doubt Ryce had something to do with the latest disappearance of T.C.'s, and she fully intended to report the man to his superiors. He'd gone too far this time, pushed her too far. And she fully intended to tell him so.

Pressing the doorbell again, Wilhelmina glanced around. At least the man didn't live in an underground hovel. The house was small and compact with a faint air of disrepair that caused her to frown. The grass was too long, and the front porch was sagging to the left a bit and she hesitated to place all her weight on it, fearing it would finally give way.

Anxious to have T.C. safely in her care again, Wilhelmina leaned on the bell again. It pealed urgently through the house, and Wilhelmina dug in her handbag and extracted the note with Ryce's address on it, checking that she had the right place. Once confirmed, she tapped her foot again and leaned on the bell.

"Where the hell's the fire?" Ryce's deep voice boomed as the front door opened with a jerk. Wilhelmina's head snapped up as her eyes connected with his. Her anger and her breath evaporated as her mouth fell open in shock.

Ryce rose like Adonis before her startled eyes. A few beads of water wove a leisurely path slowly down his broad, naked chest, staining the edge of a towel that was carelessly wrapped and knotted around his lean, muscular hips. His hair, still damp from the shower, fell with wild abandonment around his face. He looked wet and clean and so totally male it almost took her breath away.

"Well, well, well, if it isn't Willie Walker," he said humorously, leaning one broad shoulder comfortably against the door. "Did you drag me out of the shower just to inspect my...biceps? Or did you have something else on your mind?" He grinned down at her shocked expression.

Swallowing hard, Wilhelmina allowed her astonished gaze to travel another path over his bronzed skin, from the thick cords of his neck, across sculptured shoulders so wide they blocked everything beyond. His waist and hips were narrow, hidden by the terry cloth, but his legs were long and muscular and seemed to go on forever. His feet were bare and planted firmly apart in a wide-legged stance that suggested a wild, sleeping power ready to be unleashed.

"Willie?" Ryce waved a hand in front of her face. "Are you with me, here?" he inquired humorously.

Startled, her mouth snapped shut as her eyes raced up to meet his. "I . . . I . . . umm, want to talk to you. Can I come in?" she asked hesitantly, trying to gather her composure.

Flashing her a grin that should have sent her scurrying in the opposite direction, Ryce shrugged and stepped aside, giving her barely enough room to squeeze by him. She held her breath and forced her feet to get the message her mind was sending. Cautiously, she stepped around him and into the house, not knowing what to expect. At a distance the man was intimidating and infuriating. Up close—and near naked—he was downright overwhelming!

Ryce slammed the door shut soundly behind her, and Wilhelmina nearly jumped out of her shoes. She was being ridiculous, she told herself firmly. There was no reason for her to be nervous. She was not about to let a half-naked renegade get to her.

Ryce turned to face her, and his eyes locked on hers. She felt her heart tighten and then every nerve in her body curl as his glance seared through her. Swallowing hard, she cleared her throat in an effort to do something.

"I have to talk to you," she demanded, gathering some of her dwindling fury. "Now."

He sighed and dragged a hand through his hair. "So talk."

"Would you like me to wait while you get dressed?" she inquired with excruciating politeness, knowing she was more disturbed by his dress—or lack of it—than he was.

"Why?" he inquired, with a lift of his eyebrow. He glanced down at himself and Wilhelmina's eyes followed suit. His belly was flat where the towel was cinched. Her eyes stopped abruptly, and she refused to speculate on what was under the towel.

For a man who worked indoors, Ryce had the look of an athlete. Those muscles of his didn't come out of a package, she mused, still in a bit of a shock. The man was all male and looked as if he was used to doing some type of physical work. Funny, she'd never noticed any of this when he was ... dressed.

"Yoo-hoo?" Ryce prompted, his voice amused as he waved his hand in her face to break her out of her reverie. Startled, Wilhelmina looked up at him in alarm, embarrassed at getting caught staring at the man. Her face flamed as a devilish smile played across his face.

"I ... I ..." Wilhelmina ground her teeth. "I just thought you might be more ... comfortable dressed."

"Thank you, but I'm quite comfortable," he assured her, his smile going wider. "As a matter of fact, Willie, I can talk—" he winked at her boldly "—and do a whole lot of *other* things, dressed or not."

His words caused a heated warmth to cover her cheeks. She didn't need a road map to understand what other things he was referring to.

Remembering why she was here, Wilhelmina drew herself up. "Where is he?" she demanded, not bothering to go into a lengthy explanation as to why she was here and make a fool of herself. Again. Ryce very well knew why she was here.

"Who?" he inquired, glancing around the room in bewilderment.

"Don't play coy with me, Ryce," she threatened, trying to keep her mind on the problem at hand and not on his ... biceps, as he called them. "You know very well who!" Drawing herself up, she glared at him, unable to contain her fury. "If you'd kindly get T.C.," she said stiffly, "we'll be on our way."

"Get T.C.?" he echoed blankly. "Willie, what the hell are you talking about?"

His obtuseness only infuriated her. "Don't pretend you don't know anything about it, Ryce!" she yelled, her patience gone. "You know very well T.C.'s run away again. And I have no doubt you had something to do with it. Now where is he?"

"T.C.'s run away?" Ryce repeated in alarm, his tone of voice clearly indicating the news was a surprise to him.

Wilhelmina stared at him suspiciously for a moment. Was this another of his pranks? She searched his face. His blue eyes were shadowed and . . . sincere. Her eyes rounded. "You didn't know?" she breathed, all hope flying out the window. "Oh, Lord!" If T.C. wasn't here . . . Oh, God, the thought was too much for her to even consider.

"You just assumed I had something to do with it, didn't you?" Ryce growled, clearly annoyed at her accusation.

"Yes," she admitted glumly, realizing she'd tried and convicted the man without even hearing his side of it. A wave of guilt engulfed her.

"How long has he been gone?" Ryce inquired urgently, looking tortured as he jammed a hand through his hair.

"S-since this morning," she stammered, aware that she quite possibly had made a very grave judgment error as far as this man was concerned.

"This morning!" Ryce bellowed. "Why the hell didn't you tell me sooner?" he demanded, and her spine stiffened in indignation as he took a threatening step closer.

"Because I didn't know this morning," she yelled right back at him. "This is all your fault," she cried, giving his broad bare chest a good poke with her slender finger.

"My fault!" he returned, his voice rising to match hers. "Why the hell is it my fault?"

"Because you're the one who encouraged T.C."

"Are you saying it's my fault the kid likes me?" he asked, totally incredulous at her accusations.

"Yes!" she declared firmly, realizing immediately how ridiculous her answer sounded. "You knew very well I had to tell him he couldn't come to live with you," she said stiffly. "You led him on and disappointed him, and now he's run away again."

Ryce leaned forward and pressed his face close to hers. "You told him he couldn't come live with me!" he growled, his eyes blazing in fury. "What in the hell did you do that for?"

Wilhelmina shrank back. A flash of good old-fashioned fear overrode her temper. "B-because..." she stammered, totally off balance, "it's the truth."

"Of all the dumb pigheaded—" He broke off and glared at her. Wilhelmina felt a shiver race through her at the look on his face. "You tell the kid he can't come to live with me, break his heart, and then you have the nerve to show up here and tell me it's all my fault! If that isn't the pot calling the kettle black! Of all the dumb, asinine things I've ever heard, this takes the cake!" They stood still, glaring at each other for long silent moments.

"Ryce?" she finally said, her voice soft and shaky. "You really don't know where he is?" She looked at him hopefully, vividly aware that he was looking at her in much the same way she usually looked at him. Like she was out of her mind.

"No." He began to pace the entryway in short, angry steps. "You and you're damn procedures and regulations," he muttered, dragging a hand through his hair. "All you care about are your rules," he accused. "You don't care one bit about T.C., or anybody else for that matter!"

Unexpected tears began to fill her eyes. His words deeply hurt. She cared for the children, more than she would ever be able to admit. In her job, she had to maintain a cool, detached, impersonal air. If she didn't, she would never be able to function. Over the years she'd grown attached to more children than she cared to recall, and knowing that she could do little to change things, well . . . She did the best she could with what she had to work with, but she couldn't leave herself open to heartache anymore. Not if she wanted to be effective in her job. And she did do her job well.

But there was always that feeling that no matter how much she did, no matter how well she did her job, it just wasn't enough. But that didn't mean she didn't want to try. The only way she could deal with the reality of her professional life was to divorce herself from her personal emotions, at least where her work was concerned. She couldn't do her job effectively if she let her personal feelings color her professional judgment. To have Ryce accuse her of not caring was a low blow.

"That's not true," she defended, her voice shaky with tears. "I—" She swallowed around the lump in her throat. "I . . . care about the children a great deal."

"Oh hell, Willie, don't cry." He abruptly stopped his pacing and came to stand in front of her. "Don't cry," he ordered, looking like a man who had no idea what to do with a woman who did. Hesitantly Ryce reached out and touched her cheek. "I'll find him. Don't worry."

His touch was warm, and something sparked inside of her. It was difficult to get enough air in her lungs when he was standing in the same room. It was near impossible with him hovering over her.

His eyes were soft and probing, and her lids lowered to stop the rush of tears. Wilhelmina took a deep breath. Perhaps she'd been too quick to judge him, she realized belatedly. Apparently he really *did* care about the child. Otherwise, why would he be so upset?

Had she let her personal feelings for the man, her contempt for his wild ways and unorthodox methods, color her judgment of him as a prospective foster parent? Looking into his eyes, Wilhelmina realized she wasn't sure.

"Willie," he said gently, his fingers working the tender skin of her cheek and sending a heated shiver shimmying through her. "I'll make a deal with you."

His words caused her inner confusion to die, and she looked at him suspiciously. Why did the idea of making a deal with this man suddenly make her feel like she just agreed to make a deal with the devil? "What kind of a deal?" she inquired cautiously, and he laughed at the distrustful look on her face.

"Nothing as ominous as you're thinking. Here's the deal. I'll help you find T.C., if you promise to reconsider my application to have T.C. come to live with me."

"That's blackmail!" she cried, appalled that the man had put her in such a position. "And besides," she added regally. "It's your *job* to find T.C."

"And it's *your* job to find a good home for him," Ryce countered, his eyes darkening with determination. "You've ruled me out without even giving me a chance. Don't be so sure that I can't conform to the rules and regulations. I know the law. In order to be a foster or adoptive parent in this state, someone has to be at least eighteen years of age, have resided in the state for at least six months and be of sound mind and body." He grinned at the sudden scowl on her face. "Now before you make any snap decisions, I *am* of sound mind, whether you believe it or not. Just because I don't dot all my *i*'s and cross all my *t*'s doesn't mean I'm not playing with a full deck. Now, what do you say, is it a deal?"

Wilhelmina looked at him long and hard. She had a feeling he was going to look for and find T.C. regardless of whether she agreed to his deal or not. What she didn't know was if she let her personal feelings interfere in her professional judgment.

"Look, Willie," Ryce went on in a rush, "just because we don't see eye to eye on things, doesn't mean you shouldn't at least give me a fair shake. You're always nagging at me about rules and regulations. But you know very well, *you're* not supposed to let your personal feelings or prejudices interfere in your decisions regarding foster parents."

His words hit their target. What he said was absolutely true. Ryce knew as much about the rules as she did. He just happened to choose to ignore them. Wilhelmina felt an overwhelming sense of regret. Perhaps she had been unfair. Not only to Ryce, but perhaps to T.C., as well. She met his gaze, startled at the bleakness reflected in his bold blue eyes, and decided instantly that it was only fair to give him the benefit of the doubt. His deal would allow her to do that. What harm would it do to reconsider him? She would simply go through standard procedures and let the man sink—or swim—on his own merits.

None, she realized. And at least she would know that she'd done her job in an orderly and proper fashion. Just because the man drove her crazy with his rebellious way of doing things, didn't necessarily mean he should automatically be discounted as a potential foster parent, did it?

"What do you say?" Ryce cocked his head and smiled at her. "Is it a deal?" He looked at her expectantly until she finally nodded her head.

"It's a deal, Ryce," she agreed, somewhat hesitantly. "But I want you to—"

"Hot damn, Willie!" he exclaimed, grabbing her around the waist and hauling her off her feet in his excitement. He spun her around and she laughed as a delicious shiver ran the length of her. Sensations ripped through her, curling her nerves in a fierce heat. New feelings, wild pleasures engulfed her, and she found her equilibrium taking a nosedive. Breathless, Ryce's fresh, clean, masculine scent threatened to overwhelm her!

"P-put me down, Ryce," she stammered. He stopped twirling her immediately and let her slide slowly down the front of him so that she was vividly aware of his naked, muscled body. Off balance, she swayed a bit as her limbs refused to absorb the shocks her body was suddenly experiencing.

"Sorry," he said sheepishly, flashing her a smile. His eyes hovered on her mouth, and her lips parted expectantly. Tenderness etched the lines of his face, the curve of his smile. His blue eyes, once so blatantly bold, were now warm with tenderness. Ryce dipped his head toward her, and his lips parted so that she caught a flash of straight white teeth.

Frightened of him and the feelings engulfing her, she lifted a hand to his bare chest, ignoring the sizzling warmth that immediately arced between them. He stopped and looked at her for a long time. Wilhelmina tried to take a breath, to gather her composure. "I want you to know that you'll get no special treatment. You'll be judged just as everyone else. Do you understand?"

Sighing, he gave her a small smile. For the first time it reached his eyes. "I understand," he assured her. "You won't be sorry. I promise to conform to every damn rule and regulation—"

"Don't forget the procedures," she reminded him.

"And the procedures," he agreed. "All I want is a chance, Willie." He looked at her so expectantly, she smiled.

"A chance is all you're going to get," she reminded him, but her voice had lost some of it's intensity.

"Hot damn!" he said again, shaking his head in disbelief. He leaned over and kissed her gently on her cheek. Ryce drew back, looking as stunned as she by his sudden action. Abruptly his expression changed, and he turned on his heel, heading for the stairs.

"Where are you going?" she cried, too stunned by his sudden withdrawal to react. Hurrying behind him as he took the steps two at a time, Willie couldn't help but wonder what brazen thing the man was up to now.

"To put some pants on," he called, glancing over his shoulder to flash her a wicked grin. "Want to watch?"

Chapter Three

Willie, don't be ridiculous. You're not coming with me." Tugging a shirt on over his jeans, Ryce barreled down the steps with Willie right on his heels. She'd waited outside his bedroom door for him to change, despite his invitation to come watch.

"I'm not being ridiculous," she insisted stubbornly, hurrying to keep up with him. "And I *am* coming with you." Wilhelmina angled her chin defiantly. Ryce sighed and bent to pick up his boots.

"There's no reason to come," he growled, tugging on one boot, then the other. "Go home. As soon as I find him, I'll call you. Don't worry," he added gently, rising and planting his hands firmly on her shoulders. He looked at her intently for a moment. For the first time in his adult life, Ryce was scared. He didn't like the way he responded to this woman. She stirred up feelings and emotions he thought long dead and buried. He needed to put some distance between them. Soon.

"Don't you trust me, Willie?" he asked, causing her to flush.

It wasn't a matter of trust. Despite her decision to give him a fair chance, Wilhelmina still had reservations about the handsome, slightly crazy detective.

She didn't need to answer. Ryce could see the indecision in her face. "Oh, hell." Ryce shook his head and sighed. "I'm not dragging you through the streets of the city. You have no idea the places I'm going to have to go to look for T.C. I don't want you with me," he said firmly, as if the matter was settled. He yanked a leather jacket out of the closet and hurriedly stuffed his arms into it.

"You forget, Ryce," she argued, showing some of her determination, "I'm a social worker. You can't take me anywhere I haven't been before." She gave him a knowing look.

How the hell was he supposed to keep his mind on his business with her looking at him with those beautiful gray eyes? When she was around, all he seemed to be able to think about was...her. And he didn't like it, not at all.

"Don't be too sure about that, Willie," he said shrewdly, trying to harness his thoughts and emotions.

"Ryce," she said softly, her voice full of determination. "I'm coming." She was touched by his obvious concern about dragging her into parts of the city he considered unsafe, but it didn't alter the fact that she was determined to go with him to find T.C. She knew she wouldn't be able to rest until she knew the child was safe.

Willie was also certain her guilt had something to do with her determination. Ryce was right. It *was* partially her fault that T.C. had run away again. Maybe if she hadn't been so quick to tell the child that he couldn't live with Ryce, none of this would have happened.

"Can you ride a bike?" Ryce asked abruptly, pulling open the front door and heading down the walk before she had a chance to answer.

Willie frowned as she followed him into darkness. "Why?" she inquired suspiciously, her tone of voice clearly indicating that her bike-riding ability, or lack of it, was not important in the scheme of things.

"Because," he returned evasively, ducking behind a tree and causing her to sigh in exasperation.

"Well...yes," she said, stretching the truth a bit and following him around the side of the house. She hadn't ridden a bike since she wore braces on her teeth and had patches on her knees. But she certainly saw no need to point out the fact to him. Her frown deepened. Ryce might be unorthodox, but surely he didn't expect them to go bike riding around the city in the dark looking for T.C.?

"Oh, no!" she gasped as he wheeled a big, disreputable black-and-chrome motorcycle toward her. Obviously they had clearly mixed signals on the type of *bicycle* they had been discussing.

"Something wrong, Willie?" he inquired, looking up at her with a grin as he brought the machine to a stop in front of her.

She swallowed hard and inched away from him. "I...I...can't ride that thing," she stammered, her eyes going wide as her stomach performed gymnastics.

"Why not?" Ryce frowned at her, clearly not seeing the problem.

"Because..." she said blankly, willing to die before she'd admit that she was terrified of motorcycles. Let alone a motorcycle that Ryce was in control of. She was willing to do a lot for her job, but riding around in the middle of the night on a two-wheeled machine driven by a man who surely promised death or dismemberment was clearly asking too much, even for her.

"I have a skirt on," she protested lamely, trying to take another step back.

"So take it off."

Her gaze flew to his. She could barely make out his features in the dark, but she had a feeling there was a devilish smile on Ryce's lips. "I can't..." she stammered again, not knowing *exactly* what it was she couldn't do; take off her skirt or get on the bike. Willie decided she wasn't going to do either.

"Don't worry," he coaxed softly. "I'm a good driver. Now don't look at me like that. I really am." He grinned at her. "Besides, *you're* the one who insisted on coming with me." Ryce threw his leg over the bike and wheeled it toward her. Wide-eyed, she kept inching backward until he'd nearly rolled on top of her. She curled her toes for protection and pressed her back into the tree. "Come on, Willie. You've got to have a *little* trust."

Willie opened her mouth, but before her mind could form the words, Ryce reached out, grabbed her around the waist and plopped her down on the bike, totally ignoring her squeals of protest. He dropped a helmet in her lap. "Now settle down," he ordered, kicking the starter so the bike roared to life and instinctively Willie grabbed her ears and covered them.

"Willie," he yelled, cocking his head toward her and trying to be heard over the noise of the bike, "you can't hold your ears while we ride," he teased, trying to soften her fear. "You'll fall off. You've got to hold on to me. And put your helmet on!" he ordered. Grinning, he peeled her trembling hands loose from her ears, plopped the too-big helmet on her head, fastened it, then wound her arms around his waist, topping it all off with a reassuring pat.

"Now hold on," he instructed, as if she intended to do something to the contrary. He shifted the bike into gear and they roared off down the drive.

With her arms wrapped around his middle, she could feel every inch of his lean torso. Willie took one look at the ground moving fast below her, groaned softly, then buried her face against his jacket, wondering if there were any provisions in the agency budget for hazardous-duty pay.

Ryce angled the bike expertly through the streets. She couldn't see very much with her eyes squeezed partially shut and her face buried in his back. Her narrow skirt was confining and kept riding up high on her thighs. But she was too scared to worry about how much leg she was showing. At the moment she was just grateful she still had a leg to show!

Despite the warm air, the wind whipped at her face, tumbling her hair into a disorganized mess. She lifted her head—once—and quickly buried it back in Ryce's jacket with a frightened moan when she saw the flash of oncoming cars heading in their direction. She thought she felt his body shake with laughter, but she wasn't sure, and she was too scared to find out.

Whimpering softly, Wilhelmina clutched her arms tighter around Ryce. Her breath was caught by the wind, and her heart roared in her ears. She wasn't certain if the increased tempo of her pulse was from the wild ride or from the wild man she was pressed so intimately against.

Ryce shifted gears and slowed for a light, and she hesitantly lifted her head again.

"Hey, Mikey!" A man called from across the street. Wilhelmina let go of Ryce and turned in the direction of the voice. *Mikey?* Her eyes widened. She knew Ryce's first name was Michael, but she had a hard time imagining anyone calling rough, rude Ryce "Mikey." And living to tell about it. Her mouth twitched in amusement.

"Hold on," Ryce ordered, making a U-turn in the middle of the street. He reached back with one hand and grabbed her by the seat of her...skirt. Willie gasped as the touch of his fingers on such a delicate area of her body sent a shiver of excitement through her. Ryce fishtailed to a stop, obviously not in the least bit disturbed about the fact that he had his hand clasped to her bottom. Still clenching her teeth, Willie let out a breath she didn't know she was holding as Ryce released her.

"Morty, how you doing?" Ryce inquired, as the man approached. Morty was dressed in an oversize green army coat that hung limply to his ankles. The large pockets were stretched out and stuffed with what was clearly all his belongings. On his head he wore a hat fashioned out of old newspapers.

"Fine, Mikey, just fine." Morty eyed Willie, his rheumy eyes taking in every exposed inch of her. She flushed. "Very nice, Mikey. *Very* nice. Your taste is improving." Morty flashed them a toothy grin. "Got any money, Mikey?" he whispered out of the side of his mouth. Ryce stood up, apparently unaffected by his nickname, and jammed his hand into the pocket of his jeans. "Willie?" he whispered out of the side of his mouth, turning his head toward her. "Got any money on you?"

"Money?" she squeaked, still eyeing Morty, who'd pulled out a harmonica to play a catchy little tune. Absently, she reached into her skirt pocket and pulled out a twenty.

"That's too much," Ryce barked, as if she emptied her pockets to street people every day and knew just the correct amount. "Got anything smaller?" He took the twenty from her hand, crumpled it into a ball and tucked it into his jeans. Digging deeper into her pocket, she found a five and handed it to him.

"Here," Ryce said, holding up her five dollars for Morty to see but not touch. "Now, Morty, I'm looking for a kid. About eleven, dark brown eyes, brown hair. Have you seen him?"

"Can't say that I have," Morty said, shaking his head. "But I'll be sure to keep an eye out for him." He happily took the money from Ryce.

"Now, Morty, you make sure you get something to eat," Ryce ordered. "You got somewhere to stay tonight?"

Morty shuffled his feet nervously, jamming his harmonica into the pocket of his coat. "I'll find something. Don't worry about me, Mikey."

"If you run into any problems," Ryce said quietly, "you know you can crash by me." Nodding, Morty shuffled off, waving to Willie and pocketing the five.

Willie's eyes widened. She couldn't help but wonder if Ryce made a habit of opening his house to street people. Personally, the idea touched her beyond measure. But professionally, for T.C.'s sake, she felt a skitter of uncertainty about the idea. Before she had a chance to ask Ryce about the man, Ryce kicked the bike into gear, pausing to grasp her hands and pull them around him again.

"Now hold on this time," he ordered. She clenched her arms tightly around him, wondering if it was all right to be clenching all the places she was clenching. Ryce roared off again, doing another U-turn in the middle of the street as her breath was jerked from her.

His broad shoulders blocked out what little view she had, and his powerful back acted as a buffer against the wind. His scent clung to his jacket. With every shaky breath, his scent, his presence seemed to burrow deeper into her senses.

The muscles of his arms bulged and shifted as he gracefully drove the big machine. His legs strained against the pedals, relaxing only when he stopped for a light or slowly eased around a corner. Her thighs were pressed against his, her breasts flattened against his back. She could feel Ryce's body tense as she pressed ever closer, hugging him tight. If she lived through this ride, she decided, she was going to kill him!

Willie scowled at Ryce's back. What on earth was she doing, she wondered darkly. At the moment, she didn't have any money, and she was quite sure she didn't have any sense, either.

Why hadn't she just gone home and waited for Ryce to call when he found T.C.? It really wasn't necessary for her to accompany him. He had more experience finding runaways than she did. So why had she insisted on coming with him? Perhaps, she realized honestly, her reasons had to do with her feelings for the man, which weren't at all professional or impersonal.

"Willie!" Ryce's voice startled her in the sudden silence, and she reluctantly lifted her head. "You can let go of me," he said, grinning as he tried to pry her arms loose from around him. "We've stopped." His eyes danced merrily as he inspected her wild-eyed face.

"Are we still alive?" she asked tentatively, slowly unwinding her arms from around him.

"You're a good sport," he said, tenderly brushing the hair off her face.

Blinking, Wilhelmina dragged her eyes away from his and glanced around at her surroundings. Ryce slid off the bike in one fluid motion, taking her with him as he went. Her legs wobbled, and she swayed against him. His arm caught her weight, and he looked down at her carefully.

"Are you all right?" he inquired, his eyes serious and concerned. She tried to drag up a smile as she clutched her hands to her chest.

"I will be as soon as my heart kicks in again. I think it stopped about six miles back."

Laughing softly, he dropped an arm around her shoulder. "See that warehouse over there?" She looked where he pointed, and frowned. The neighborhood was dark and seedy and consisted mostly of empty buildings and burned-out warehouses. She was used to being in declining neighborhoods, but most of them had been occupied by houses or apartments with plenty of people visible. She had to admit she'd never ventured into a decaying business neighborhood in the dark of night where there were more empty buildings than people. A shiver of fear raced through her.

"I see it," she confirmed, nodding her head and inching just a bit closer. She would worry about her pride later, right now she was too scared to worry about anything but saving her hide.

"I'm going in there," he told her, causing her to glance up at him.

"Alone!" she cried in alarm. She didn't know which scared her more, the idea of staying out here by herself, or Ryce going into that building. Alone.

Ryce laughed softly. "Willie, you forget I'm a cop. I'm used to going into all kinds of dangerous situations. Now stop frowning like that. I've done it hundreds of times before." He cocked his head and let his eyes rest on hers. "Don't tell me you're worried about me?" he asked, his eyes so reverent her knees grew weak. He couldn't remember the last time someone—anyone—had been worried about him. It felt . . . good . . . scary.

"I sure am," she retorted, feeling uncomfortable because she *was* worried about him and she didn't know why. "I don't know how to drive that blasted thing!" she quipped, motioning toward the bike and hoping she'd successfully hidden her more-than-professional feelings for the man.

"Now, Willie, listen carefully. Some of the gangs use that abandoned warehouse for a clubhouse. I'm going to go in there to see if anyone's seen T.C. I want you to stay here, and don't move. Understand?" he growled. "Now, there's a horn on the bike. Right here." He grabbed her hand and guided it toward the horn. She tightened her fingers on his, and a heated shiver rolled over her. "If anything happens out here, you lay on that horn. You got it?'' He looked at her and scowled. "You got it?'' Ryce repeated firmly.

"I've got it,'' she assured him weakly, her eyes darting around.

"Are you sure you'll be all right?'' Ryce inquired, his scowl deepening. He cursed himself. He should have listened to his better judgment and not brought her along. But, damn, he couldn't bear the thought of leaving her alone to worry and fret about T.C. He would rather have her with him, for more reasons than just the ones he was admitting.

"Now don't move from here,'' he instructed gruffly, as if she planned a neighborhood tour. He gave her hand another reassuring squeeze.

"I won't,'' she said, knowing that she was too frozen with fear to go anywhere. Turning on his heel, Ryce checked his gun and then strode toward the building.

"Ryce?''

He turned to look at her, walking backward as he went. "What, Willie?''

"Be careful,'' she called, lifting her hand in a half wave and giving him a tremulous smile.

"I have to,'' he said, flashing her a grin and giving her a thumbs-up signal. "You don't know how to drive the bike, remember?'' Another shiver raced through her as she watched him round the corner and enter the building.

The dark grew oppressive; it surrounded her like a thick cloak of doom. Willie's senses went on red alert. Her eyes adjusted quickly, and she nearly screamed when she saw a rodent scurry across some garbage in a nearby alley.

She cocked her head and tried to listen, but all she could hear was the rapid pounding of her heart, which seemed magnified in the quiet darkness of the night, echoing loudly in her ears. A faint breeze wafted through the air, filling her with an ominous chill. Where was Ryce, she wondered, straining to see better. He'd been gone so long.

Standing practically on top of the bike, she tried to keep a harness on her fear. But a frisson of hysteria shot through her. She had only seen Ryce as an unorthodox, undisciplined cop. She'd never really given any thought to this part of his job, the dangerous part. He always seemed poised on some craziness, so that at times she forgot that there was another, dangerous side to his life. There seemed to be a lot of sides to Ryce. He was like a diamond, with many facets that her natural curiosity cried out to explore. Time seemed to stop, and she grew more nervous for Ryce.

"Well, well, well, what have we got here?" The unfamiliar male voice caused her to whirl around. Her heart nearly pumped right out of her chest at the sight of the trio of boys. As they sauntered closer to her, she saw that the boys weren't much older than fifteen or sixteen, but the menace in their eyes, on their faces, made them look much older indeed. She shivered in fear.

"Such a pretty little thing," one of the boys caroled, as they circled the bike, coming even closer to her.

One boy, the largest of the trio, reached out and slid his finger down her cheek. Willie shrunk back from him, as stark terror rose like bile in her throat. Oh, God, why hadn't she listened to Ryce? Why had she been so pigheaded about coming with him?

"Touch her again, Jimmy," Ryce growled from behind, "and I'm going to change your channel for you!" Wilhelmina's shoulders slumped in relief at the sound of his voice. Her eyes met his, and she saw another Ryce, one that was tough...frightening. The look on his face was enough to scare her out of her boots, had she been wearing them.

"Oh, hell, it's you, Ryce," the kid called Jimmy complained.

"Willie?" Ryce's voice was soft as he slid a hand around her neck and guided her toward him. "Easy," he soothed, drawing her closer and sliding his arms around her. "Easy." He could feel the tremors of fear shake her slender frame, and a fierce protectiveness rose up inside of him.

Willie clutched the front of Ryce's shirt, leaning against him. Burying her face in his chest, she savored the scent and safety of him.

"Willie, are you all right?" Ryce gently caressed the back of her silky head. She nodded, unable to stop trembling.

His hard body was pressed against hers, and despite her fright, she couldn't help but feel every chiseled muscle of the man.

"Jimmy," Ryce said, his voice cold and frightening, "if you touched her..."

"We didn't do nothing, did we, boys?" Jimmy glanced at his companions, who hung their heads. In an instant, the sauntering, confident boys had changed into frightened, quivering kids. "So, Ryce, what's up?" Jimmy asked, shifting his jean-clad frame nervously.

Ryce stared at the trio long and hard. "I'm looking for a kid. T.C. Sherlock. He's about eleven, dark brown hair, brown eyes. Have you seen him?"

Three pairs of eyes exchanged sheepish glances. It was Jimmy who spoke up again. "We ain't seen no one who looks like that. Have we, boys?" The other two shook their heads in agreement.

"If you do," Ryce went on coldly, "you'll let me know, won't you, boys?" It wasn't a question, but a quiet, harsh command. The playful, arrogant man was gone, replaced by the tough cop.

"We sure will," the trio agreed in unison, slowly backing away from Ryce.

"Be sure you do. Good night, boys," Ryce said, clearly indicating the conversation was over and their presence no longer welcome. The boys shuffled off, and Willie felt some of her fear subside as Ryce held her tightly for a long moment.

"Dammit, Willie," Ryce growled, settling his hands on her slender shoulders and holding her away from him so he could see her. "Are you sure you're all right?"

Tentatively she lifted her head. Silently she nodded, as his eyes carefully went over her.

"I should never have agreed to take you with me," he growled, cursing his own stupidity. "It's too dangerous. The next time I tell you to stay put, you're *going* to stay put. Got it?"

He could still feel her shaking, and he cursed himself for putting her in danger. Damn! He knew better. A civilian, and a woman at that, was a handicap he couldn't afford.

"Why the hell didn't you lay on the horn?" he inquired gently, not letting her go just yet. If it had been anyone other than Jimmy and his gang, they could have both been in trouble.

"I froze," she answered truthfully, lifting her large frightened eyes to his. Ryce sucked in his breath. She looked so beautiful, so vulnerable.

He lifted a finger and traced the line of her brow. His touch was so unexpected, so gentle, her breathing grew ragged again, not with fear this time, but with something so unexpected, her eyes widened.

He slowly slid his finger down to touch her eyelids, her cheek, dropping to outline her lips. She stared up at him with fearful gray eyes, torn between wanting him to stop and wanting him to continue. She felt something drawing her, tugging her, closer to him, and she was powerless to stop it. Her lips parted expectantly, waiting, anticipating.

"Willie," he whispered, cradling her face in his hands. She looked like a fawn caught in a hunter's sight. He felt something stir deep inside, and he worked quickly to banish the feeling. *Too close.* She was getting too close to all the barred off places inside of him. Ryce shook his head, trying to shake off the feelings. Wilhelmina Walker was dangerous. She could get to him. And he *couldn't* and *wouldn't* allow it. He had to keep a tight rein of control on his feelings and emotions.

Damn, this woman could do things to him with just a look, he thought in disgust, dropping his hands and taking a step back.

"Let's get out of here," he said gruffly, cursing himself up and down for his lack of self-control. "I'm taking you home."

"My car's at your house," she reminded him as she slid her arms around his waist again and settled herself on the bike. Her arm brushed against his gun, and she shivered.

"Then I'll take you to my house. I want you to get in your car and go home. You stay put," he added, to forestall any objections she might have. "I'll find T.C. I promise. But I want you safe at home."

Hanging on to him for dear life, Wilhelmina nodded, then lowered her face, pressing it close to his jacket as Ryce roared through the streets. The man was as complex and confusing as one of those colored cubes. Just when she thought she had him figured out, he showed her another side. Why did he keep withdrawing from her? Why did he keep closing himself off?

Her thoughts sped as fast as the bike. Vividly aware of his body where it pressed against hers, Willie tried to keep her mind on the problem at hand, finding T.C.

It was difficult to keep her thoughts where they belonged with Ryce so close and her mind in such confusion.

Ryce slowed the bike and downshifted as he climbed the driveway of his house. He drove around the side and turned off the ignition. Grateful that the evening's fiasco was over, Willie started to pull her arms from around him, but Ryce stopped her. Without a word, he slid his hands over hers and held on.

Too stunned to say anything, Wilhelmina sat there, letting the warmth of his hands seep into hers, knowing instinctively how difficult it was for a man like Ryce to reach out to someone. But he'd reached out to her, and she found herself warming toward him, feeling things that had nothing to do with her job or her professionalism.

Finally, sighing deeply, Ryce released her hands and slid off the bike. His eyes met hers, and for a moment she saw something in his eyes, something rare and very real. It caused her breath to quicken. Ryce reached out and dropped his arms around her waist, gently lifting her off the bike and setting her down.

"Come on," he said softly, "I'll walk you to your car." The darkness engulfed them. Silently, they walked down the sidewalk that led to the front of the house.

"Ryce!" The voice came out of nowhere, and before he had a chance to react, T.C. flung his body at Ryce, nearly knocking him to the ground.

"What the hell?" Ryce dropped to his knee, and his arms automatically went around the boy. "T.C., where the hell have you been?" Ryce held the boy away from him. The child's liquid-brown eyes brimmed with unshed tears and Ryce's heart went cracking against his ribs. "Are you hurt?" Maybe the child wasn't hurt physically, but Ryce knew from experience the hurt T.C. was feeling went deeper than any physical pain. He slowly inspected the boy. Except for a few scrapes and bruises along his face, T.C. looked all right.

"No," T.C. answered, swiping at his dripping nose with the sleeve of his shirt. "I ran away—that lady, Ms. Walker—she told me—she told him—" A sob broke loose. "She said I couldn't come and live with you."

"I know," Ryce whispered, hauling the sobbing child close. "I know, T.C.," he said gently, his arms tightening in comfort. "But that's no reason to run away."

"I'm scared, Ryce," T.C. whispered, his voice cracking with emotion.

"Don't be scared, T.C.," Ryce ordered gruffly, feeling his own heart constrict. Ryce's eyes slid closed, and the years rolled away. His mind saw another boy, older than T.C., but just as frightened and just as alone....

"I'm scared," Michael had whispered into the darkness.

"Don't be scared. You'll be all right."

"Stay with me," Michael had pleaded, so frightened he couldn't think straight.

"I'll stay with you," his father had promised. "Don't be scared. I'm here. I'll take care of you...."

But he hadn't. Pretty words. Empty promises. Ryce's jaw hardened as the memories flooded him. Just a kid, but he'd been left alone with nothing but his tarnished innocence and his ragged fear. Fear that haunted him to this very day. On that night so long ago Ryce had learned to hide and control his emotions, to barricade himself against any further pain.

It was a hard lesson, but one well learned. He'd forced himself to hide his fear behind a devil-may-care, cocksure attitude. Never again would he be that innocent, that vulnerable. Never again would he allow himself to care about someone. Caring meant letting go, being vulnerable. It meant giving up control of yourself and your emotions to someone else. Giving them the power to hurt you. That night, oh so long ago, Michael Ryce had vowed that no one would ever have the power to hurt him again. *No one.*

"Ryce?" T.C.'s voice jerked Ryce back to the present. He blinked, banishing his own memories.

T.C. looked up at him, his eyes full of tears and hopelessness. "I'm s-scared," T.C. whispered again, and Ryce swallowed hard, feeling the burning sting of pain behind his eyes.

"Don't be scared, T.C. I'll take care of you," Ryce said softly, repeating the words that had been said to him so many years ago. He tightened his arms around the trembling child. Ryce vowed no matter what it cost him, no matter what the price, *his* words, *his* promises *wouldn't* be empty.

T.C. looked up and saw Wilhelmina. His eyes filled again, and his trembling increased. "Are you sure?" T.C. asked hesitantly, and Ryce nodded his head.

"I'm sure," Ryce said, wanting only to reassure the child and erase the ragged fear from his eyes. "I'm going to take care of you T.C. And I promise you," he went on, his eyes finding Willie's over the top of the child's head, *"nothing or no one is going to take you away from me!"*

Chapter Four

Nothing or no one is going to take you away from me.

Willie shook her head as Ryce's words echoed through her mind. If only it was as simple as a promise. Easing herself down on the shaky front steps of Ryce's porch, she sighed heavily.

Ryce had taken the sobbing T.C. inside with a promise to return as soon as he had the child calmed down. *Promised.* A faint smile curved her lips. She wasn't quite sure if it had been a promise or a threat. It was clear that once again she was the enemy. Despite the cautious truce they'd declared earlier in the evening, Willie knew that the camaraderie between her and Ryce had now been forgotten. The battle lines were clearly drawn, with her on one side and Ryce on the other.

Why, she wondered, was he suddenly treating her like the enemy again? Hadn't she told him she would reconsider his application for custody of T.C.? Obviously Ryce thought *reconsider* and *approve* meant the same thing. But that certainly didn't entitle him to make a promise to the child that he wasn't sure he could keep.

Sighing heavily, Willie brushed a few wayward strands of hair off her face as a faint breeze gently rasped against her face. She inhaled deeply, enjoying the sweet summer air.

At least one of her questions had been answered. Apparently Ryce really did care for the child. Despite his aura of arrogance and indifference, despite his brashness and pugnaciousness, when it came to T.C., Ryce's feelings were quite clear.

While Ryce may not care much for rules and regulations, she knew without a doubt that he cared a great deal for T.C.

But caring about a child just wasn't enough, Willie thought sadly. She still wasn't convinced about Ryce's commitment not just to T.C., but to parenting as well. Raising a child was a full-time job, an enormous responsibility. She had a legal, moral and ethical responsibility to make sure that T.C. was placed in the best possible foster home.

Willie rested her chin on her hand. Then there was the matter of Ryce's peculiar way of dealing with things. She couldn't just forget the man's unorthodox and wild ways.

Despite her attempts to remain detached and professional, she knew she was drawn to Ryce in ways that weren't in the least bit detached and professional. But she couldn't let her personal feelings about the man interfere in her professional judgment. Not against him, nor in his favor. Her first responsibility was to T.C. She had to remember that, and keep her personal feelings out of it. She had to keep a clear head about her shoulders in order to make a rational decision.

"Willie?"

She jumped as Ryce's husky voice shattered the evening stillness. Taking a deep breath, she turned her head to look at him as he pushed open the screen door and stepped outside. He'd shed his jacket and unbuttoned the collar of his shirt. Just the sight of him caused her breath to quicken. With Ryce standing above her, she had to tilt her head to look at him. It was an unfair advantage, she decided.

"Is T.C. all right?" she asked, totally baffled by the look on Ryce's face.

He looked distant, closed off. The muscles in his jaw were tense, and he deliberately looked away from her questioning gaze, lowering his eyes to the toe of his shoe.

"Fine," he said curtly, his voice clipped and cold. Ryce jammed his hands in the pockets of his jeans and walked down the steps. Willie watched him in silence, wondering what kind of private demons he was fighting and if they had *her* name on them.

Ryce turned to her but remained silent. Willie lifted her gaze to his, expecting him to be his old arrogant, cocksure self. Her eyes widened a fraction. Ryce's eyes were now hooded and tormented. Something tugged at the soul of her heart.

Ryce stared at her, trying to control the feelings and memories that were overwhelming him. Damn! He was too damn old to be hurt by youthful memories. He wanted to tell her, to explain, but the words wouldn't come. He'd never been very good at verbalizing his feelings. He'd buried them so long ago, that now it was difficult to open up to someone—anyone. But if he wanted T.C.—and he did—he would have to open up to Willie.

"You ever been alone, Willie?" he finally asked, hooking one booted foot over the bottom step and rocking it to and fro. Ryce's voice was soft and low, yet Willie detected the ever-present thread of steel running through his tone.

"Alone?" She smiled. "Plenty of times. I was just alone while you were inside."

He laughed bitterly, the sound echoing hollowly in the night's stillness. "No honey, I mean *totally* alone."

Willie looked up at him, realizing he'd meant something else. Alone. As in all alone with no one to turn to, no one to care. No, she'd never been alone, at least not that way. Even though she lived thousands of miles away from her parents now, she always knew that her family, their love and their support were always as close as the phone. It was a safety net she'd never really thought about. Until this moment. Someone was always there if she needed them. It gave her a peaceful, secure feeling that no matter what went wrong in her life, she had a family; parents, grandparents, brothers and sisters who loved her and were always there to back her up.

"No, I guess not," she said quietly.

Ryce nodded, turning his back to her to stare off into the distance. A police siren whined mournfully in the night. Silent seconds ticked by.

"You have no idea what it's like to know you're all alone in the world," Ryce finally said, his voice shattering the silence. "To know that there's not one damn person who cares whether you live or die." He turned back to face her, his jaw tense, his eyes bleak. "That's the way T.C. feels," he said, dragging a hand through his hair.

Willie's eyes searched his face. She had a feeling Ryce wasn't just talking about T.C., but she didn't want to push him. She was going to let him say what he had to say in his own way, at his own pace. Perhaps—just perhaps—she would grow to understand him a little better.

Ryce dropped down next to her. Close enough for her to feel the warmth of his body, but not close enough to touch her. "When I was eleven, my mother died."

"I'm sor—" He cut her off with a wave of his hand, clearly indicating he didn't want her sympathy. Willie fought back the feeling of being rebuffed.

"My stepfather—well, I never thought of him as my stepfather. He was the only father I'd ever known. I thought the sun rose and set on the man. It was tough when my mother died, but I still had Al, still had his love." Ryce leaned back against the stairs, crossing his legs in front of him.

"One night I had a nightmare. I woke up and was scared to death. Al came into my room and sat with me. It was odd, because I never had nightmares. But Al stayed with me until I fell asleep. When I woke up the next morning, he was gone. He'd stripped the apartment of everything of value. I never saw him again," Ryce said quietly, his deep voice low and controlled. "I guess he didn't want to be saddled with someone else's kid."

Willie's heart ached for the young boy Ryce had been. To be betrayed by someone you loved and trusted hurt at any age, but to have it happen when you were just a child was horrifying. She wanted to reach out and touch him, to comfort him, but she didn't. She had a feeling he wouldn't accept her comfort. "What did you do?" she asked quietly.

"Do?" Ryce shrugged negligently, as if the memories didn't matter. But Willie knew they did: "For the first few weeks, I went to school, came home and just pretended everything was normal. I kept thinking he'd come back." He paused. "After a few weeks I realized he was really gone. Pretty soon I ran out of money. The landlord was screaming about the past-due rent, and I had to eat, so I started stealing. Little stuff, just enough to feed myself. I got caught. As soon as they found out I was an abandoned, under-age child, they sent me to a group home." Ryce finally turned to look at her. The pain in his eyes caused her soul to ache. "Do you know what that's like?" he asked. Ragged fear and his memories rose up to engulf him. Ryce struggled for control.

Willie shook her head, not trusting herself to speak.

"It's a large place where they house supposedly 'bad kids.' I lived there with sixteen other boys, all different ages. We had two adults who lived there and supervised us. Bastards, both of them," he bit out, his voice hardening. "They treated us like criminals. They never gave us an ounce of kindness. They had us labeled as no-good, and they treated us as such. You know the old saying—a kid behaves the way you expect him to. Well, that's exactly what those two guys did. We got a beating for the slightest infraction of the rules. Those guys seemed to take some kind of sadistic pleasure out of scaring and controlling helpless kids. We didn't have the rules and regulations that are in place now. Those guys were the law and were left to do whatever they wanted." Ryce's fists clenched at his side, and Willie suddenly understood Ryce's need for control. If *he* was in control, no one could ever hurt him.

"What about adoption?" she inquired softly, restraining herself from reaching out to him.

"Adoption?" Ryce snorted derisively. "Some things never change, Willie. I had a stepfather somewhere, remember? He was my guardian so legally I couldn't be adopted. Not that anyone wanted to adopt an older kid who was known as a troublemaker. Besides, everyone wanted cute little babies, and I was a far cry from cute or a baby." His words were bleak, and Willie ached to reach out to him, to comfort him, but she didn't.

"I stayed in that group home until my eighteenth birthday. Then, they packed up all my belongings in a paper bag, gave me twenty-five dollars and sent me on my way." He stared off into the distance, and a vein in his temple throbbed ominously. Willie ached for the lonely, vulnerable child he had been and the hard, closed-off man he had become.

"Ryce?" Unable to contain herself any longer, she hesitantly reached out to cover his hand with hers. She'd expected him to shrug her off, but he didn't. Ryce allowed her hand to rest on his, then slowly linked his fingers through hers and squeezed gently. Willie slowly let out her breath.

Ryce glanced down at his hand entwined with Willie's. He couldn't remember the last time someone warm and gentle had comforted him. It was an odd feeling. Yet at the same time, it was nice. Had it been anyone else but Willie, he would have shrunk back. There was something different about Willie, something warm and special, despite her rigid ways. Something about her seemed to touch the cold wall he'd built around his heart. It frightened him with an unknown emotion he couldn't seem to name.

"You have nice hands," he said softly, giving her hand another squeeze and lifting his gaze to hers. There was a faint smile on his lips as the warmth of his body seeped into hers.

"Thank you," she whispered a bit self-consciously. Their palms were resting against each other. Her tender skin pressed against the rather roughened skin of his. It was an odd mixture of contrasts, different and exciting. His hand dwarfed hers. While her skin was a pale, milky white, Ryce's skin was a dusky bronze, dusted with flat whorls of dark, curly hair. His hand was warm and welcoming.

"Willie?" He had to explain to her why he'd told her about himself. Not because he wanted her sympathy or pity. All he wanted was her understanding. And not for himself, but for T.C. Maybe if she understood why T.C. meant so much to him, she would understand why he wanted custody of the child.

She swallowed hard at the way he said her name. She lifted her gaze to his. The pain was gone now, replaced by a reverent tenderness that filled her with an odd, slightly off-kilter feeling.

"*Now* do you understand why T.C. means so much to me?" he asked quietly, and she nodded.

"I think so." He tightened his fingers on hers in acknowledgement.

"T.C. is right where I was at before I went to the home. He's been labeled as a troublemaker through no fault of his own. In his mind, all he's done is try to survive in a world that he feels has no place for him.

He's frightened and alone. He's been alone so long that it's second nature to him now. That's why he keeps running away from those foster homes. He doesn't feel like he belongs anywhere. Do you know what that feels like? How empty and worthless it makes you feel?'' Ryce shuddered inwardly, vividly recalling the feeling.

Willie nodded, suddenly understanding. Ryce wanted to give T.C. something he himself never had, acceptance, security, love.

"T.C. trusts me, Willie. Don't you see, I'm his last hope. I've seen enough kids like T.C. to know they don't give their trust very often. Sometimes never. *But he's given his to me,*" he said firmly. "I want to reach him before it's too late. You can help me do that." Ryce stopped and waited for her to look at him. "Willie, I became a cop because—well—" he gave her a sad, empty smile "—despite the hell I went through, I thought maybe I could help other kids avoid the same pain. But, hell, I've been in the system long enough to know that I can hardly make a dent. It's not like I haven't tried. Believe it or not, even though I don't follow all the rules and regulations, I do care about my job. And about the kids," he added softly. "But it's like a damn revolving door. There's not enough hours in the day. Too many kids, too little time, too few homes." Ryce shook his head. "Years ago when I was young and naive, I actually thought I could make a difference. Kind of like you."

Willie suddenly understood why he was always giving her such a hard time about the rules, regulations and her requirements of strict adherence. Ryce believed that no matter what she did, it wouldn't make a difference. What he didn't know was that she felt she

had to at least try. And not just because it was her job.
But because she felt it was the right thing to do.

"I know better, now, Willie. I didn't think I'd ever
be able to say I could make a difference. But T.C.'s my
chance. If I can make a difference in his life, show him
that someone does care, that he's worth something to
someone, give him a place where he knows he belongs, hell, maybe then the past fifteen years won't
have been wasted after all. He means a lot to me, Willie. A lot." Ryce stared off into the distance, and Willie nodded.

Her heart warmed toward Ryce. She wanted to
reach out, enfold him in her arms and take away his
pain. Underneath his rough exterior Ryce was a man
fighting his own years of emotional pain.

No wonder he'd fought her tooth and nail the past
few weeks. No wonder he handled things in such an
unorthodox manner. Ryce probably saw her as an authority figure. The one person who stood between him
and T.C. And she really couldn't blame him. She'd
come on entirely too strong, been entirely too judgmental of him. Ryce probably saw her rejection of him
as just another in a long line of rejections. A wave of
remorse engulfed her. How could she have been so
blind, so uncaring?

Perhaps, she mused, it was because from the moment she met Michael Ryce she knew he'd been different from any other man she had met. She'd reacted
to him in ways that made her uncomfortably aware of
her own femininity. As a result, she'd lost all shred of
objectivity. But that certainly didn't excuse her un-
professional behavior. She had let her personal feelings, or rather her *fear* of her personal feelings,

interfere with sound professional judgment. She'd never allowed that to happen before.

Ryce was what he was; he didn't pretend to be something he wasn't, and he didn't put on airs. He was brutally honest, and when he wanted to be, also warm and caring.

It was an odd contrast, and not at all what she expected. She'd just assumed he was a certified crazy who drove her nuts just for the pure pleasure of it.

But now she knew better. From what Ryce had told her, she knew that he would never ask to take the child into his home if he wasn't willing to make a permanent commitment. She'd prejudged the man and condemned him without giving him a fair hearing.

Maybe Ryce didn't dot all his *i*'s and cross all his *t*'s—as he put it—but she no longer doubted his sincerity or his integrity, at least not where T.C. was concerned.

"Willie?" Ryce squeezed her hand. His voice was low, and just a bit shaky. She glanced up at him, wondering how she could undo the damage she'd done. Without meaning to, she had rejected Ryce just like everyone else in his life had done. She'd hurt him just as surely as if she'd taken a knife to his vulnerable heart. "I've never asked anyone for anything." He spoke slowly and deliberately, measuring each word until she understood the seriousness of the moment. "I've got a hell of a lot of pride that I'd rather choke on than swallow. But pride isn't going to do T.C. much good." He paused to take a deep, ragged breath, and Willie found herself holding her own breath in anticipation. "I want—no, I *need* your help to get permanent custody of T.C."

Her eyes flew to his. She knew how much it cost him
to ask.... He was a loner, both physically and emo-
tionally. Asking for help was almost to admit weakness, to let go of control. Her admiration for him
grew. He must care a great deal about T.C. to make
that kind of sacrifice.

"Will you help me, Willie?" he asked, his eyes
searching hers.

Willie's breath quickened, and she found herself
totally disarmed. No matter how hard he tried to hide
it, rude, rough Ryce was a warm, caring, man, with a
lot of love to give to someone. Ryce would be the kind
of man who may not love often, but when he did, it
would be wholeheartedly. She found the thought
warmed her deep inside.

What would it be like to have this man's love, she
wondered. Her breath caught as the thought grew
stronger. Her eyes tenderly traced his features, and she
could hear the sudden thudding of her own heart in
the stillness of the night. A breeze filtered through the
air, washing her senses in the pleasure of Ryce's masculine scent.

He mistook her silence. Ryce's mind warred with
itself. Perhaps he had revealed too much to her. Perhaps too little. Hadn't he learned? *Never* let them
know what you are thinking or feeling. If they didn't
know they couldn't hurt you. Hell, it was too late to
rectify it now. What he had to do was try to salvage the
situation.

"Willie, let me explain. I'm not asking you to break
any of your damn rules or regulations," he growled,
"and let's not forget your procedures. All I'm asking
is for you to help me conform to the rules. I'm not
saying it's going to be easy. As everyone says, it's hard

to teach an old dog new tricks. Especially *this* old dog, who never liked the damn tricks to begin with. But I sure as hell will try. I'm willing to do anything to get custody of T.C." His blue eyes, so big and so blue, flickered with hope as they met hers. He waited, watching her.

She felt the tension in him as he waited for her answer. "Yes," she finally said, throwing caution to the wind. These were extenuating circumstances, she reminded herself. While, in a professional sense, her actions might not be considered correct, personally, nothing had ever felt so right.

In that instant she knew there was no way she could remain cool and detached with this man. She was already involved with him in ways that frightened her, personally involved with her heart and her mind with an intensity that shocked her sensibilities.

There wasn't anything she could do about it now. It would be like closing the barn door after the horse was out. Ryce had gotten to her. She should have been frightened. But she wasn't. Exhilarated maybe, but not frightened. What would it take to get a man like Ryce to trust, to love? Willie didn't know. But she wanted to try to find out.

She was in too deep to back out now. She had a responsibility to T.C., and whether her decision was based on personal or professional reasons, at the moment she truly felt Ryce and T.C. belonged together.

She looked deep into his eyes, feeling lost. "Yes, I'll help you," she said, squeezing his hand reassuringly.

Ryce's breath came out in a rush. For the first time in memory he felt an overwhelming sense of...of what? It felt like happiness, but he really wasn't sure he knew what happiness was. All he knew was that for one brief moment, whatever he was feeling over-shadowed the fear and loneliness he'd carried around like a heavy backpack. Ryce squeezed Willie's hand. His eyes pinned hers, sending her silent messages she wasn't sure she was reading correctly. "Thanks, Willie."

Oh, what this man could do to her heart, she thought dully, unable to drag her gaze from his.

"So...Willie, where should we start?" He grinned rakishly at her. The mood was broken, and Ryce was back to his old charming self.

Willie blinked, trying to break the spell she was un-der, trying to drag her thoughts back to a profes-sional level. She took a deep breath. "The first step is to make arrangements for you to have temporary cus-tody of T.C. on an emergency basis. Then—"

"Can you do that?" he asked with a frown. He knew what a stickler she was about rules and regula-tions. He didn't want her putting her job or her integ-rity on the line for him. All he wanted was her help. He sure didn't want her to compromise her principles.

"Sure," she said with a smile, touched that he was concerned about the propriety of things. Maybe rude, rough Ryce wasn't so rude or rough after all. "Right now," she went on, "T.C.'s in an emergency-care fa-cility. All I have to do is put through the paperwork, and he'll be assigned to your care on an emergency basis. But, in order to make it official, you'll have to meet all the requirements of a foster parent." What she didn't tell Ryce was he had already met the re-quirements as far as she was concerned. He cared for the child, was willing to assume responsibility for him and wanted to provide a safe, secure home for him. "Your house will have to meet all the requirements for a foster home, too." Willie turned to look at the house and frowned, realizing how much work needed to be done. She hadn't really seen the inside, just the foyer and the hallway.

"Honey, that's going to take some doing." Ryce whistled softly, his eyes following the direction of her gaze. "I bought this house last year, and I haven't done a single thing to it. Hell, I don't even have any furniture, unless you count one raunchy lawn chair I've got in the living room."

"Don't you have a bed?" she asked with a frown, wondering just how unorthodox the man was.

"A bed?" Ryce's eyes lit with unholy amusement. "Why Ms. Walker—" he drew back and did his best to look shocked "—I certainly didn't think an unmarried lady like yourself would be the type to be interested in my...bed." Her face flamed as he leaned close to whisper in her ear. "Willie, I've got a wonderful bed," he said suggestively, his sultry voice heating her senses. "It's big and soft and—"

"R-ryce," she stammered, giving him a playful poke in the stomach and wondering just what type he thought she was. "I was only concerned about T.C.'s sleeping arrangement. Where is he going to sleep?"

"Oh." Ryce deliberately looked dejected. "He's on a cot in one of the spare rooms right now."

"That's one of the first things we'll have to do. T.C. needs to have his own space."

"That won't be a problem, Willie. I really haven't had the time to decorate the place before. Not that I even cared to. This place was never a home to me, just a place to crash."

"Well, first thing on the agenda is to get some furniture. Don't worry," she rushed on at the look on his face. "I'll help you. It won't be that bad. We'll get some furniture and some paint. The house needs some repairs, but I'm sure we can fix or repair anything that needs it. After that, we'll have to concentrate on the actual day-to-day care of T.C. You'll also have to enroll him in school and then find someone reliable to stay with him while you're on duty."

"I don't think either of those will be a problem," Ryce said, pleased this arrangement was going to work out so well and so easily. "The school is less than three blocks from here and I shouldn't have any problem finding someone to stay with T.C."

She nodded, glad that Ryce wasn't put off by the prospect of rearranging his life for T.C. That was a good sign. "Can you cook?" she asked, trying not to grin at the look of horror that crossed his face.

"Cook?" he echoed, looking decidedly uncomfortable. He reached up to rub his chin with his free hand, and Willie's grin widened.

"Yes, you know, pots and pans, a stove, that sort of thing?"

"I've got the pots and pans and the stove," Ryce said with a frown. "But it's what you're supposed to *do* with those pots, pans and stove that worries me."

"Don't worry," Willie said with a laugh. "We'll get you a microwave, and some cookbooks, and you'll be in business."

He cocked his head to look at her, his eyes dancing with mischief. "Does this mean you're not going to teach me how to cook?"

Willie shook her head. "I—I can't," she stammered.

"Why? Is that against the rules or something?" Ryce asked, looking clearly confused.

"No, it's not against the rules. It's just—well—I can't . . ." Her voice trailed off. "Cook," she finished lamely.

"Willie!" Ryce's voice dropped to a scandalized whisper. "Are you telling me that an educated, scholarly woman like yourself doesn't know her way around a kitchen! I'm shocked." He nudged his shoulder affectionately against hers, and a tingling warmth ran the length of her. When Ryce dropped his arrogant, pompous facade, he could be quite endearing. Willie cautioned herself not to lead with her heart but with her head. She had the sinking feeling it was a bit late for that.

"Ryce, I know my way through and around the kitchen—as in going around it to get to another room. It's when I try to do things *inside* the kitchen that I get into trouble."

"Poor Willie," Ryce said with a chuckle, squeezing her hand again. "Sounds like T.C.'s not the only one who needs someone to take care of him."

Something in his tone caused her to look at him. The thought of having someone—a man—take care of her had never really occurred to her. There was a difference between *needing* to have a man take care of you, and *wanting* a man to take care of you. The idea of Ryce taking care of her—or rather, the thought of them taking care of each other suddenly sounded appealing.

Startled at the train of her thoughts, Willie rechanneled her attention to the problem at hand. "Let's see now, we've got the house, school and meals taken care of." She counted each item off on her fingers. "Once

we find a sitter for T.C., we should be pretty well set."
She smiled at Ryce, suddenly feeling very right about
her decision not only to help him, but to give him
custody of T.C.

"Willie, listen, I've got about five weeks of vacation time saved up. I think I'll call in tomorrow and
put in for time off. What do you think? School doesn't
start for about three weeks, and until T.C. gets adjusted to living here, I think it might be a good idea to
spend some time with him. It's not going to be easy.
T.C.'s spent a lot of time running wild. He hasn't
really had to answer to anyone about anything." Ryce
chuckled softly. "Boy, is that going to change."

Willie had a feeling Ryce was going to be a stern
taskmaster. Fair, but stern. "I think that's a good
idea. As long as you can afford the time, I think it
might really help. You know, Ryce, it's going to take
T.C. a while to trust you. He's going to test you every
way you can think of. I know from experience."

Her words caused Ryce to laugh. "Honey, you forget I've been a cop for fifteen years. I've dealt with
kids in every kind of situation." He cocked his head
to look at her. "Knowing my background, do you
really think T.C. can put anything over on me?"

"He's going to try, Ryce, and you're going to have
to be ready to deal with it. You're not only going to
have to provide him with love, stability and security,
but with discipline as well. It's a big responsibility."

"I know," he said seriously, looking totally un-
daunted at the prospect. "He's going to get love, affection and attention, but he's also going to have to
live within the rules I set up for him. No kid of mine
is going to be running the streets or running wild."

No kid of mine. The words reverberated in Willie's head. Ryce had already staked claim to T.C. in his heart and in his head. She felt a wave of affection for Ryce. She felt certain now she'd made the right decision. T.C. was one lucky child. On the other hand, she sure didn't want to be around when he decided to test Ryce's patience. She had a feeling T.C. was going to be toeing the line like he'd never done before. It was going to be very interesting to watch.

"Still," she continued, wanting Ryce to face the reality of the situation. It wasn't going to be all sunshine and roses. "It might not be easy to convince him that *this* is his home and that he's going to live here permanently."

"Don't worry, I'll convince him," Ryce said, his tone leaving little doubt. "Willie, now that we've got that settled, I mean after I get temporary, emergency custody, then what happens?"

"After I've done the initial investigation of you and your home, I pass my recommendation to the *guardian-ad-litem* of the county. He's an attorney who looks out for the welfare of the children in the state's custody. It's really just a formality. Once I give my approval of you and your home, the guardian will approve your application. A child has to be in a foster home for six months before adoption proceedings can begin. Since T.C.'s an orphan with no living relatives, there shouldn't be any problem."

"But first I've got to get past you, right?" Ryce smiled at her, and Willie bit her lower lip. If he only knew he'd already gotten past her. But she couldn't very well tell him that, especially after the fuss she'd put up about how unsuitable he was. Oh, how wrong she'd been!

"Right," she said finally, smiling mysteriously.

He glanced down at her hand again, still entwined with his, and a soft look crossed his features. "Looks like I've got my work cut out for me," Ryce said with a wicked sigh.

Willie smiled tenderly. "Once your formal application is approved, T.C.'s yours."

"Forever, right? Nothing or no one can take him away from me?"

"That's right."

Ryce's face broke into a wide smile. "Hot damn, Willie! I've got it made in the shade." She laughed at his obvious euphoria. She had a feeling it wasn't going to be as easy as Ryce thought. But they would take things one step at a time.

"Say, what are you doing tomorrow?"

"Tomorrow?" she repeated with a frown.

"If you don't have any plans for the weekend, I thought maybe you could come over and we can get started on the house. I'd like to get this show on the road. The sooner I get things organized, the sooner I'll know T.C.'s mine."

Willie felt a tingling rush roll over her at the prospect of spending more time with Ryce. It didn't matter what the circumstances, she realized. She just wanted to be with him. "Tomorrow's fine," she agreed. "I don't have any plans."

He cocked his head to look at her, his eyes curious. "No hot dates?" he asked mischievously.

She drew back to give him what she hoped was a stern look. "Detective Ryce, an unmarried lady like me? I'm shocked. Think of my reputation." Her words caused him to chuckle softly. He was so different when he was relaxed, she thought, feeling her senses respond to the man. Instantly, Willie was on her guard. She had to keep this on a professional level.

She made a move to untangle her hand from Ryce's, but he held tight. "If I'm going to come back in the morning, I'd better get going." Willie didn't relish the thought of leaving Ryce and going home. But she knew for her heart's sake, she'd better, before she got so deeply, so personally involved she wouldn't be able to keep her objectivity, and she needed to for T.C.'s sake. She must never forget that the child's welfare was her primary concern.

"Willie?"

"Yes?"

"There's just one more thing," he said softly, letting his fingers caress hers until her skin rippled with pleasure.

"What?" she asked, trying to ignore the sensations storming her body, blotting out her thought patterns.

Ryce was silent for a long moment, his eyes searching hers relentlessly. "Thank you," he said finally, his deep voice husky with emotion.

"You're welcome," Willie responded softly. Their eyes locked in silence.

Ryce ached to reach out and brush the errant strands of hair away from her delicate skin. She looked so fragile with her hair all tousled and clothing all mussed. Quite a difference from the woman who'd stormed into his office that morning looking for his hide.

A thrill, hot and quick, seared his blood.

Willie felt her breath wither at the look on Ryce's face. Her eyes widened in barely concealed astonishment. Ryce's big, bold eyes caressed her.

"Willie," he whispered, lifting their entwined hands to tug her closer. "I want to..."

"What?" she whispered, anticipation searing her body with aching need. "You want to what?"

Holding her gaze, Ryce leaned close until nothing but his face filled her vision: the beautiful, sad eyes, the arrogant nose, the full, sensuous, tempting mouth.

"...to taste you," he whispered a moment before his lips covered hers. Hesitantly, his mouth grazed hers, gently exploring, as if waiting for her acceptance. Or rejection. Willie slid her free hand around his neck and gently drew him closer, wanting to let him know that he would find no rejection in her arms. Her body ached with the need to touch him, a need that had been born so many weeks ago when she'd first laid eyes on him.

Her lips greeted him, welcomed him. Ryce groaned softly, the sound wrenched from somewhere deep inside. He wrapped his powerful arms protectively around her as he enfolded her tightly in his embrace. He held her so tight, she almost couldn't breathe. His lips burned into hers, claiming her, possessing hers until she didn't care whether she took another breath or not, as long as she could remain in his arms.

Hesitantly, his lips parted, and Willie eagerly accepted his gently exploring tongue as it furtively touched and tempted her waiting mouth. When his tongue gently touched hers, she slid her hand up his muscled forearm, urging him closer. Ryce groaned again, tightening his arm around her and boldly possessing her with his own masculine stamp.

Willie moaned slightly, filled with so many sensations of pleasure her heart thudded wickedly beneath her breast. She tightened her arms around him, drawing him closer until she felt the hardness of his chest pressed intimately against her.

He moved his hands gently, reverently, from her waist up along her back, finally coming to rest at her neck where he cradled her head, softening the crushing blow of his kiss.

Waves of contentment washed over her, filling her with an inner peace she'd never known was lacking until this very moment. She threaded her fingers through the heavy silk of his hair, wondering how she'd ever existed without this pleasure, this man, before.

Ryce's mouth moved urgently against hers. A mounting rush of pleasure engulfed him as an inner peace seeped into his cold heart. For the first time in memory he felt a glimpse of contentment. In Willie's arms he felt like he'd come . . . home.

Home.

The word crashed against the cobwebs of his mind, and he wrenched his mouth free. *Home.* The word reverberated through his brain, and his eyes jerked open. Regret and caution engulfed him, dousing the feelings of pleasure that had rambled leisurely through his body.

He'd known Willie was different from the moment he'd laid eyes on her. Now he knew why. He was vulnerable to her, out of control when she was near and in his arms. *He couldn't let that happen.* He'd worked too hard for control to let it slip through his fingers for a few moments of pleasure. Hadn't he learned? He didn't belong anywhere. Not in Willie's arms. Not in her heart. *He had no home.*

Stunned at Ryce's abrupt withdrawal, Willie drew back. Self-consciously she ran her tongue over her lips, tasting the lingering sweetness of him.

"It's late," Ryce said briskly, rising to his feet. "I'll walk you to your car."

Willie stood up and followed him down the steps toward her car. She didn't know what had caused his sudden withdrawal from her. And right now she wasn't sure she wanted to know. It hurt too much.

He opened her car door. "Good night, Willie. I'll see you in the morning."

Nodding, she climbed into the car and started the engine, feeling just a bit sad and forlorn. She put the car in gear and started to pull away, but Ryce's voice stopped her. She rolled down the window.

"What?" she called, turning back to see what he was hollering about.

"Fasten your seat belt," he ordered gruffly, and Willie smiled. Maybe she'd touched him—even just a little—in the same way he touched her. She did as he asked and drove home.

Only time would tell.

Chapter Five

Willie, is that you?" Ryce yanked open the front door and stared at her dumbfounded. "Come on in here. Let me have a good look at you." As he tugged her through the open doorway, Willie tried not to flush at the look of pleasure on his face.

This morning she'd traded her standard work uniform of white blouse and tweed skirt for something a bit more casual. The pristine blouse had been replaced by a soft peach shirt belted snugly over faded, well-worn denims that displayed her long legs to their best advantage. Her low-heeled pumps had been replaced by comfortable leather sneakers. She'd left her dark hair loose and flowing so that it cascaded down her back in silky waves.

Whistling softly, Ryce walked a circle around her, his eyes shining in appreciation. Willie fidgeted uncomfortably, trying to remain still under Ryce's intense visual inspection.

In her heart, Willie knew her reasons for dressing this way had more to do with the man walking a circle around her than her need for comfort. She felt like preening under Ryce's obvious approval.

He didn't look so bad himself. He was dressed in faded jeans that were threadbare in spots, and an open-collared shirt. His feet were bare, and his hair fell in a rakish tumble across his forehead.

Ryce's gaze warmed as it slid slowly over her again. A wicked smile curved his lips. He'd been right about her legs, they were long and incredibly sexy. And her hair... Lord, a man could get lost in it. It was a glorious blue-black, with the gleam of a million fiery black diamonds. Even without her dander up, Willie Walker was one beautiful sight to behold. She nearly took his breath away.

"Hot damn, Willie," Ryce said with a smile. His mouth curled in pleasure, and Willie couldn't help but remember the touch of those lips on hers last night. Hot shivers of delight raced down her spine. "You sure can brighten up a morning," he said.

"Th-thank you," she stammered, feeling flustered and pleased. They stood staring at each other, their eyes locked.

"Where's my manners?" Ryce finally wondered, shaking his head and taking her by the hand. Her pulse quickened at his touch. "Come on in. T.C.'s still sleeping. I was so excited last night I woke him up to tell him the news. I told him all about our plan."

"Plan?" Willie repeated, coming to a halt in the living room. Her eyes scanned the room. Well, Ryce had been right about it being empty, she thought in amusement. There wasn't a stick of furniture or a scrap of draperies. One badly battered lawn chair sat

remorsefully in front of a cold, empty fireplace. She
took stock of the room again. The carpeting was a
muted gray, but the room was expansive, with great
possibilities. She couldn't wait to get started.

"Yeah, our plan," Ryce reiterated, tugging her
along from the living room and through a swinging
door.

Willie came to an abrupt halt and swiveled her head
in every direction, trying to take in and categorize the
chaos in the room. If she had to guess, she would say
it was the kitchen. But one couldn't be sure. The sink
was filled to capacity with dirty dishes and pots; they
overflowed the sink and spilled out to cover every
square inch of counter space. A plastic garbage can
was filled to the brim, and a stack of newspapers were
spread across the kitchen table, along with a pile of
empty fast-food containers. One of the four mis-
matched chairs was toppled over, the four legs stuck
up in the air as if begging to be rescued.

"Now, Willie," Ryce said in a rush at the look on
her face, "it's...it's...not as bad as it looks."

Willie swallowed convulsively. No, it was worse. For
someone who was as fastidious and meticulous as she,
the sight before her was almost treason. But she forced
a pleasant smile to her face, reminding herself not to
be judgmental.

Ryce dropped her hand and hurried to clear a spot
at the kitchen table and right the chair. "I just haven't
had much time," he went on lamely, bending to pick
up some garbage off the floor and stuff it back into the
already too-full can. "I've pulled a lot of extra hours
this month, and with going to school, I just don't seem
to have any time for...cleaning." He said the word as
if it were totally foreign to him. From the looks of his

kitchen it might as well have been, Willie thought humorously.

"School?" She asked absently, rolling up her sleeves. With a determined gait, she marched across the kitchen and began to empty the sink. The first thing she had to do was clear away some of the debris so that she could restore some order to the place.

"I'm going to night school," Ryce said evasively, causing Willie to stop and turn to look at him.

One brow rose in question. "For what?"

He shrugged, looking decidedly uncomfortable. "It's no big deal, Willie. Just wanted to take a few extra classes to further my education." He was busily folding the newspaper and scooping the empty containers off the table. With his arms full, Ryce aimed the containers at the garbage can as if he were shooting baskets. The containers scattered all over the floor.

"Guess I need some practice," he said sheepishly, and Willie turned to hide a smile.

She had a feeling there was more to the few-extra-classes-to-further-my-education story Ryce was giving her. But at the moment, she decided to let it drop. She wanted to go slow. She didn't want to push him. He had to open up to her on his own, without her prodding. She could wait. If only she could keep her curiosity intact. There was so much about him she didn't know, but longed to know... Like how he managed to get himself from an eighteen-year-old kid with only a few dollars to his name to the police force. But she would wait. There'd be plenty of time.

"Come sit down, Willie," Ryce said, trying to steer her away from the sink. His hand was warm against her skin, and she felt her heart scamper a bit at his nearness. "There's plenty of time for that. Can I get you something?"

Her lips twitched. "A broom and some disinfectant might be nice," she teased, and Ryce threw back his head and laughed. The sound rumbled around the room, warming her heart. He had a nice laugh, she thought, wondering why he didn't laugh more often. She dropped into the chair he pulled out for her.

"How about some coffee?" Ryce offered, and Willie looked at him skeptically.

"You know how to make coffee?" she asked, using the same tone of voice she would have used if he'd just offered to make an atom bomb.

"Nope. I know how to boil water," he admitted with a crooked smile, crossing to what she hoped was the stove. He picked a jar up off the counter and waved it in her direction. "These little coffee crystals do the rest." Ryce filled a pot with water, waited for it to boil, then poured the steaming water into two paper cups before heaping a large dollop of instant coffee into each one.

"Here you go, Willie. Just like downtown." He set a cup in front of her, and Willie resisted the urge to check the steaming brew for critters doing the backstroke. Ryce was trying so hard to be hospitable, she couldn't very well be insulting. Glancing around the room again, she said a silent prayer and then cautiously sipped her coffee. The fragrant smell caused her stomach to rumble ominously. She'd been so anxious to get here this morning, so anxious to be with Ryce again, she hadn't bothered with breakfast.

She'd tried to tell herself it was all part of her job, all part of the excitement of placing a child into the right home. But in her heart, she knew her feelings about seeing Ryce again were more than professional. *Much* more.

"You should have seen this place before I straightened up." Ryce blew on his steaming coffee and took a sip, watching her over the rim of the cup. His eyes twinkled mischievously at the look on her face.

"You...straightened up in here?" She nearly choked on her coffee.

"I did," he assured her, glancing around the kitchen and grinning lamely. "I guess maybe I need a cleaning lady."

"No," Willie retorted, enjoying his lighthearted mood. "I think a demolition squad is what you need."

Ryce laughed. "That's good, Willie. You know, you're pretty nice when you're not so full of—"

"Detective Ryce," Willie scolded, shaking her head at him. He smiled, and their eyes met. Stunned at the intensity of her own feelings, Willie lowered her gaze and sipped her coffee in silence.

"So, Willie, what do we do first?" Ryce asked, watching her curiously. "Where do we start?"

We. How could such a harmless word make her feel so wonderful? Perhaps it was because the *we* in this case was comprised of her and Ryce. Willie attempted to keep her wayward thoughts under control.

"The first thing *we* have to do is get this place cleaned up," she said firmly, sweeping the room with a glance.

"From the tone of your voice, Willie, I've got a feeling you've just become the field general in charge of KP detail." Ryce smiled, obviously delighted with the idea.

"I'll be the field general, but every general has troops. You and T.C. can help." Ryce groaned at her suggestion, but she saw the humor dancing in his eyes. "Now, tell me about the rest of the house?"

"Are you sure you want to know?" Ryce asked, chuckling at the traumatized look on her face.

"No," she assured him. "But you'd better tell me anyway."

Ryce tilted his head to look at her. His eyes were shining, making them seem even bluer and bolder in the morning light. "It's a pretty standard house. There's a living room-dining room combination. You saw that on the way in—"

"The empty rooms, right?"

Ryce nodded. "This is the kitchen, in case you didn't recognize it," he added. "There's a half bath on the first floor and a full bath and three bedrooms upstairs."

"But just one bed, right?" she inquired mischievously, remembering their conversation from last night.

"There you go again, Ms. Walker, always got your mind on my bed." Ryce shook his head and clucked his tongue. "Would you like to see it?" he whispered, leaning close to her and doing his best to leer. "Or maybe you'd like to try it out?"

Willie burst out laughing. "Thank you, but I'll pass. I've lived this long without seeing your bed, and after seeing your kitchen I don't think my heart can take any more shocks today."

"Pity," Ryce teased, his voice dropping to a suggestive whisper. "It's really a *very nice* bed." He drew the words out until her face flamed. "I'd be happy to give you a personal tour."

"What else have you got upstairs?" she said, determined to change the subject.

"Nothing," he said simply, draining his cup and then aiming it toward the garbage can. He missed again. "But don't worry, I've got some money saved. I thought we could go out shopping for some furniture. I'm not much good at that sort of thing. I've already talked to my commander, and as of this morning I'm on vacation. I'm all yours," he said with a smile, and Willie's heart flipped over.

All hers. The thought brought an unexpected lift to her spirits. She had a feeling Ryce would never be all anybody's. Anytime someone got too close for comfort, he pulled back and retreated. But still, the thought warmed her. Ryce was a challenge; she couldn't help but find him intriguing.

"Ryce! Ryce! Where are you?" T.C.'s voice sounded on the edge of panic, and Ryce jumped from the chair.

"I'm in the kitchen, T.C.," he said quickly. Noting the look on Ryce's face, Willie knew he wanted to reassure T.C. that he was still there, that he hadn't left him.

T.C. bounded into the room, a wide grin on his face. Willie smiled. His brown hair was mussed, a cowlick stuck straight up in the air. His jeans were torn and patched, and his shirt had more holes than material. A collection of freckles dotted his turned up nose, and his brown eyes glowed with happiness. Despite his almost Huck Finn appearance, Willie knew T.C. was always about five minutes from trouble.

T.C. came to an abrupt halt when he spotted Willie, and the smile slid off his face. "What the hell is she doing here?" he demanded, his tone of voice sour enough to spoil milk.

"T.C.!" Ryce barked, his voice firm and low. "Watch your mouth. That's no way to talk to Ms. Walker. Or in front of her." Ryce glanced at Willie, who ducked her head to hide a smile. She'd told him it wasn't going to be easy. Maybe now Ryce would realize he had his work cut out for him. But looking at the two of them, she knew T.C. was worth every single bit of effort. "I want you to apologize to Ms. Walker right now."

T.C. looked from one adult to the other. Tension, silent and deep, hung in the air. It was the first battle of wills between T.C. and Ryce, and Willie shifted uncomfortably. She had no doubt about who would win this particular battle, but she had a feeling T.C. wasn't quite sure. She hoped he wouldn't push Ryce. Perhaps the child didn't know him as well as he thought.

She really couldn't blame the child for his resentment. After all, she *was* the one who had told T.C. he couldn't live with Ryce. It was natural for the child to resent her. But she was certain once T.C. realized that she wasn't the enemy and that she wasn't there to hurt him, but to help him, his animosity would ease.

"T.C.," Ryce thundered, his deep voice booming around the room. He seemed unwilling to wait for his orders to be carried out.

"I'm sorry," the boy grumbled half-heartedly, not bothering to hide his contempt.

Ryce smiled gently. "That's better, T.C. Now, Ms. Walker is going to spend some time with us. Remember, I explained all that to you last night."

T.C. nodded, deliberately averting his eyes from Willie's.

"The first thing we have to do, T.C., is get some furniture for your bedroom."

"My bedroom," T.C. repeated excitedly. "You mean I'm going to have my own room?" His face shone with pleasure, and Willie felt her heart tug. Obviously the kid never had a room of his own. Or anything else.

"Well, you sure as hell aren't going to sleep with me." Ryce laughed, reaching out to ruffle the boy's hair. Ryce's eyes met Willie's over the top of the child's head, and she smiled in understanding. The first weeks after a child was placed in a home was a tension-filled time both for the adults and the children. Neither really knew what to expect. But they would learn. Together. This was going to be a new experience, for T.C. and for Ryce. She was glad she was going to get the chance to be a part of it. Perhaps she might be able to ease some of the tensions she knew would crop up between them.

"Got any cola?" T.C. asked, bounding across the room to open the refrigerator. He pulled out a can of cola, popped it open and took a long swig. Willie frowned and caught Ryce's eye. She shook her head, nodding toward T.C.

"T.C., cola's not exactly on the breakfast menu." Ryce crossed the room and pulled the can of cola away, dumping it down the sink.

"But I *always* have a cold one for breakfast," T.C. protested, glaring at Willie as if he'd read her silent signals to Ryce.

"Not anymore you don't," Ryce confirmed. "You're going to start eating and drinking like a normal kid. Three squares a day, and plenty of sleep."

"Jeez," T.C. complained with a long face. "What a drag. You sound just like one of those parents on television." The words hung in the air. T.C. looked at Ryce. Ryce looked at T.C., and Willie held her breath waiting, watching them. Finally, the child's face broke into a wide smile. "I ain't never had a parent," T.C. said in a tone of awe. Willie felt a lump in her throat and swallowed hard.

"I know," Ryce said softly. They just stood there looking at each other. Finally, Ryce cleared his throat. "You'd better get used to it, kid. From now on, you toe the line. No more running the streets or running wild. And *no* smoking," he added firmly, as T.C. pulled a crumpled pack of cigarettes out of his pocket and prepared to light one. Ryce snatched the pack out of T.C.'s hand and tossed it toward the can. He missed again.

"Now go get dressed, and don't give me any lip about being dressed. You look like a ragamuffin. There's a brand-new pair of jeans on my bed from the last time you stayed here. There's a shirt, too. We'll stop and pick you up some clothes this afternoon. You'll need some new clothes for school, anyway."

"School!" T.C. cried in horror. "You mean I gotta go to school, too? Come on, Ryce, only nerds go to school."

"So you'll be a nerd." Ryce laughed at the look on T.C.'s face and dropped an arm affectionately around his neck. "Get going now. Get changed. We've got a lot to do today."

"No cola, no smokes," T.C. grumbled as he sauntered out the kitchen door. "And on top of it, school. Jeez, Ryce, all this clean living will probably kill me."

* * *

"Six weeks," Ryce bellowed, scaring the timid salesman nearly out of his shoes. "I can't wait six weeks for this furniture. I need it now!" Ryce's deep voice boomed around the furniture store, and the thin salesman mopped his brow.

"I'm sorry, sir," the salesman stammered, looking helplessly at Willie.

"Would you excuse us a moment, please?" Willie inquired, taking Ryce firmly by the arm and steering him into a corner. "Ryce," she scolded. "You can't yell at the poor man like that. You nearly gave him a heart attack."

Frowning, Ryce turned to look at the man, then turned back to Willie again, flashing her a sheepish smile. "Hell, Willie, I didn't mean to scare him. But who ever heard of waiting six weeks for furniture. If I needed it in six weeks, I'd have waited six weeks to come and get it. Now what are we supposed to do? T.C.'s got to have a place to sleep. Did you see how excited the kid was about his new bedroom set. How am I going to tell him he has to sleep on a cot for the next month and a half?"

Willie tapped her finger absently against her lip. "Maybe you won't have to. Come on, I've got an idea. But you let me handle it. You've scared that poor man enough for one day." With Ryce in tow, Willie went back to the salesman, who looked like he was searching for a place to hide. She put on her biggest smile. "Excuse me, do you have a warehouse around here?"

The man brightened. "Why, yes, as a matter of fact, we do. If you could arrange to pick up the furniture from the warehouse, you could have it today. Providing everything's in stock." He glanced hesitantly at Ryce. "It's just that our deliverymen are so overloaded. It's not that we don't have the furniture, you understand. We just don't have enough men for deliveries, so everything is delayed.'' He mopped his damp brow again. ''Summer is such a busy time. You have no idea the problems we— Well, I'm sure you understand,'' he said hopefully.

''I understand,'' Ryce assured him, deliberately making his voice sound less threatening. ''Where's this joint at?''

''Joint?'' The man swallowed hard, glancing at Willie.

''The warehouse, sir,'' she explained, giving Ryce a good poke in the arm. ''Where is it located?''

''Oh, the warehouse.'' He smiled in relief. ''It's in Geneva, about an hour from here. If you like, I can give them a call right now so that everything will be ready for you.'' The salesman hurried away, looking quite relieved.

Ryce was frowning, craning his neck in every direction. ''What's wrong now?'' Willie asked in exasperation.

''Have you seen T.C.?'' Ryce asked worriedly. ''Where is that kid? He said he was going over to the stereo section. I don't like him wandering around by himself.''

Willie smiled. Ryce had already staked a claim to the child, and he was now behaving like an overprotective mother hen.

''You go ahead and look for him. There's something I have to do.'' She'd seen something in the accessory shop she wanted to buy for Ryce, but he hadn't left her side since they walked into the store two hours ago. And what a two hours it had been! They'd selected a living-room set, a dining-room table and chairs with a matching credenza, a new kitchen table and a complete bedroom suite for T.C. In a span of two hours Ryce had spent several thousand dollars. He kept assuring her he could afford it all, but still she was worried. She knew a cop's salary didn't allow for many luxuries. But Ryce actually seemed to be enjoying their spree. She had a feeling it was the first time Ryce had ever shopped for furniture. He'd told her his house wasn't really a home, but just a place to crash. Maybe now both T.C. and he would see it as a real home.

After securing her purchase, Willie went back to the salesman's office. He hurried out to her.

"Everything's set. You can pick up everything but the credenza for the dining room. It's out of stock, but they expect to have it in about three weeks. You can pick it up at that time."

Nodding, Willie took the card with the address of the warehouse out of his hand and headed off to the stereo department to find Ryce and T.C. They were both hunched over an enormous stereo speaker, deep in thought.

"What on earth are you two doing?" she asked with a laugh.

"So what do you think, Ryce?" T.C. asked, deliberately ignoring her. Willie let it go. There was no point in trying to force the issue of having T.C. acknowledge her. She just had to give him time. She was certain he would come around. Eventually.

"I think it's a lot of money," Ryce admitted, and T.C.'s face fell. "But what the hell," Ryce said with a smile. "We'll need something to play music on when you have your friends over. Right?"

"Friends?" T.C.'s face hardened, and he looked dejected. "I ain't got no friends, Ryce."

"You've got me, kid," Ryce said gently, throwing an arm around the boy's shoulder. "And Willie." He glanced over at her, and Willie couldn't help but notice the dark scowl that etched T.C.'s face. Quite clearly he didn't exactly see her as a friend. "That's all you need for now. Let's go see if we can find that salesman and tell him to throw in the stereo, too." Ryce looped his other arm around Willie. *If looks could kill,* she thought, noting T.C.'s expression as they set off in search of the salesman.

Once the paperwork had been done and Ryce had written a check, they headed outside to Ryce's car.

"Willie, why don't you come with us to pick up the furniture?" Ryce opened the front door for her, but T.C. pushed past her and scrambled into the front seat. Ryce started to say something, but Willie put a hand on his arm to stop him. All T.C. was doing was staking out his territorial claim to Ryce. It was a natural act, and she would have to make Ryce see it as that.

"It's all right," she said for Ryce's ears only. "I'll sit in back. I'll explain later," she promised, climbing into the back seat.

Muttering under his breath, Ryce walked around his side of the car and started the engine. "So what do you say, Willie. Do you want to come with us? I thought maybe we could stop for lunch." He was grinning at her in the rearview mirror, giving her that look that never failed to melt her resistance.

"I'd love to, but I think you'd better drop me off at the house. I'd like to get the place straightened up a bit before you bring the furniture in."

"That sounds like a great idea," T.C. enthused, looking more animated than she'd seen him all day. "Ryce, you and I can go together to get the furniture. Besides," he said, turning to slant a glance at Willie, "she doesn't look like she'd be much help anyway."

"T.C.," Ryce growled, "that's just about enough. I won't have you talking to Ms. Walker like that, or treating her like that. It's about time you learned how to act around civilized people." Ryce met Willie's eyes in the mirror again, his eyebrows raised in supplication. She smiled, acknowledging that she understood.

T.C. was silent while Ryce kept up a running commentary until they stopped at a grocery story. Willie left them in the car and went to buy cleaning supplies. When she returned, Ryce bounded from the car and hurried to relieve her of her bulging bags. She didn't miss the roll of T.C.'s eyes or the look of disgust on his face at Ryce's helpful gesture. Winning T.C.'s trust and confidence was going to be about as easy as waterskiing down a waterfall.

After Ryce dropped her off and went in search of a truck to rent, Willie set about cleaning the kitchen. One of the first things she was going to encourage Ryce to buy was a dishwasher, she thought when she was well into her third batch of dirty dishes. For a man who had a fondness for paper dinnerware, he sure had a lot of dirty plates. And for a man who couldn't cook, he had a lot of dirty pots. How one man could dirty so many kitchen articles, she would never know.

Once the sink and counters were spotless, she rolled up her sleeves, filled a bucket with hot, soapy water and set about washing the floor. The tile was a neutral shade of beige, and quite attractive once it was clean. She couldn't wait to set the furniture in place.

There was a knock at the back door, and Willie pushed herself to her feet to answer it. Expecting Ryce, her eyes widened at the sight of Morty.

"Hi, Billie," he said with a grin and a salute, looking just as scurvy as he had last night.

"It's *Willie*," she corrected. Lord, she thought in disgust, now Ryce had *her* using that blasted nickname. No one but Ryce had ever called her anything but Wilhelmina. No one else would have dared.

Morty shifted uncomfortably, looking past her into the house. "I saw Mikey a little bit ago. He told me to come over here and wait for him. I guess I'm going to help him move some furniture?" He didn't sound too sure of himself, but Willie let him in anyway. If he knew about the furniture, he'd had to have seen Ryce. Besides, there was something rather sweet about Morty.

"Be careful of the floor," she cautioned. "It's wet."

Morty came to an abrupt halt and slipped off his battered tennis shoes. "Don't want to mess up your floor," he explained with a toothy smile. He picked his shoes up and tiptoed across the floor in his holey stocking feet.

"Have a seat," she instructed, touched by his gallantry. "I'll be finished with this floor in a minute." She knelt back down and dipped her rag in the soapy water again.

Morty watched her with intense interest, frowning and clucking occasionally. Finally, he stood up, peeled off his overcoat and laid it carefully over a chair. "Billie," he said, gently taking her hand and helping her to her feet. "An elegant lady like yourself shouldn't be on her knees scrubbing floors. Let me do it." Too mystified at his actions, Willie didn't bother to correct his pronunciation of her name this time. "I'm an old pro," Morty told her, slowly getting to his knees to begin cleaning. "I used to own a restaurant."

She glanced at him, surprised by his admission. "What happened to your restaurant?" she asked politely, suddenly curious about the gentle old man.

Morty shrugged, not bothering to stop scrubbing. "After Timmy came back from the war—he was my son—anyway, he had a lot of medical bills. Had to sell the restaurant to pay them." He paused and looked forlornly at the floor. "Timmy died," he said quietly. "Didn't see any reason to bother with anything after that." Smiling sadly, Morty ducked his head and continued scrubbing.

"I'm so sorry," Willie offered, feeling a bit of the old man's pain. Now she understood why Ryce had such an affection for the old man. Some people took in stray animals. Ryce seemed to attach himself to stray people. It was a touching trait, and she found herself all the more intrigued by rude, rough Ryce, who no longer seemed so rude or so rough.

Morty looked at her and smiled. "Oh, don't be sorry, Billie. It's not so bad anymore. After a while the pain goes away." He chuckled heartily. "I know I don't look so good. Don't smell so good, either. But I'm harmless. Mikey, he kind of looks after me. I know I can always crash with him or get a few bucks from him to get something to eat. He's a nice boy, that Mikey. Real nice." Morty looked at her carefully. "You like him?" There seemed to be a great deal of significance attached to his question, and Willie measured her answer appropriately.

"Yes," she said slowly, wanting to reassure him. "I like him."

Morty smiled, obviously pleased. "He's not much for people. Kind of a loner. Seems to like kids, though. Had that young'n in the car with him when I saw him before. Said he was going to adopt him."

Willie nodded. "Ryce is going to adopt T.C. That's why I'm here," she explained. "I work for the Children's Welfare Agency. It's my job to find homes for children in the state's care."

Morty was silent for a moment. "Well, Mikey will give the boy a good home. He's a cute kid. Kind of reminds me of Timmy." Flashing her a sad smile, Morty bent over and began scrubbing again.

Sensing he wanted to be alone with his memories, Willie stood up. "As long as you're doing the floor, I think I'll make myself useful somewhere else in the house." Morty nodded, and Willie went off to clean the rest of the first floor. Before she was done, she heard Ryce's car in the driveway. She'd opened all the windows in order to air the house out, and Ryce's booming voice filtered through the rooms.

"Yo, Morty, come give me a hand!"

"Coming, Mikey." Morty hurried through the house, propping open the front door as he went to help Ryce. Willie followed behind.

"Put it over here," Willie instructed, throwing a dish towel over her shoulder as she directed the positioning of the furniture.

It took almost three hours to unload the rented truck, but when they were finished, the house looked wonderful. Groaning, Ryce, T.C. and Morty collapsed on the couch.

"I'm pooped," Ryce admitted, rubbing a cramp out of his arm. "Thank goodness I don't have to return the truck until tomorrow. How about some dinner?" he asked of the collected group.

"That depends," Willie said skeptically. "Who's cooking?"

Morty sat up. "I'll cook," he offered with a smile, and Willie and Ryce exchanged meaningful glances.

"There's really nothing in the house," Willie admitted, making a mental note to take Ryce grocery shopping. "We've got a microwave, but no food to put in it."

"I can run to the market," Morty decided, getting to his feet. "It's better if I do the shopping. I'm real particular about the kind of ingredients I use. Don't need no fancy oven, either," he said with a bit of scorn. "I prepare meals the old fashioned way," he sniffed indignantly. "I cook them!"

"Can I go with Morty?" T.C. asked excitedly, pulling himself up from the couch. Willie and Ryce again exchanged glances. Morty and T.C. seemed to have formed a mutual admiration society.

"Sure, go ahead," Ryce agreed, anxious to have a few minutes alone with Willie. They hadn't had a chance to talk all day, with all the running around they'd done. He wanted to have a chance to thank her for all she did. And to try to explain T.C.'s hostility. She was one special woman, he thought, looking around the house.

"Let's get going, kid." Morty grabbed his ever-present overcoat. Willie made a mental note to ask Ryce why Morty insisted on wearing the coat in this heat.

Ryce stretched to dig some money out of his pocket. "Here, Morty, get something real special, something to celebrate." His eyes met Willie's. Tonight he felt like celebrating.

"I know just the thing," Morty said with a grin, stuffing the money in his pants pocket. "Come on, kid."

They started off toward the door. Morty looked at T.C. and said, "By the way, what's the *T* in T.C. stand for?"

"Timothy," T.C. said with a snort. "Do you believe it? What a nerdy name."

Morty glanced at Willie over his shoulder. "His name's *Timmy*," his eyes seemed to say.

"Well, Timmy," Morty drew the boy's name out, rolling it over his tongue and savoring it, "I have a feeling we're going to get along just fine. Yep," Morty said, flashing Willie a wink and throwing an arm around T.C., "just fine, son."

Chapter Six

I didn't know being a parent was so backbreaking."
Ryce groaned, rubbing the back of his weary neck and
stretching out his long legs.

"This is just the beginning, Ryce," Willie said with
a knowing laugh. Laying her head on the new chair,
she glanced around the room and smiled. The room
looked wonderful. The furniture they'd chosen was
warm, comfortable and definitely masculine. Muted
shades of brown and gray sprinkled with beige domi-
nated the large couch and matching wing chairs.

She glanced over at Ryce. He'd let down his guard
a little bit and no longer seemed quite so hard or intimidating. Surprisingly, she felt very relaxed in Ryce's
company. Willie had really enjoyed herself today—
despite all the hard work. And she'd enjoyed spending time with Ryce. A small smile curved her lips.
Spending time with Ryce could become habit form-
ing.

He lifted his head and looked at her. "So...what do you think?"

Willie frowned. "About what?"

"Now, Ms. Walker," Ryce scolded in his best policeman's voice, "don't be obtuse. How do you think my first day as a parent went?" It was clear from the expression on Ryce's face that he wasn't just fishing for a compliment. He sincerely wanted to know if she approved. She was touched that her opinion seemed to be so important to him.

"You did great," she said, meaning it. "It's going to take some time, Ryce. You can't expect miracles Both you and T.C. have been alone for a long time. It's not going to be easy living with someone else, being responsible for someone else. You're both going to need time to adjust, not only to each other but to the situation."

Ryce sat up, looking decidedly uncomfortable all of a sudden. "Willie... I don't know what's gotten into T.C. I'm really sorry about the way he's been treating you—"

"Don't worry about it," Willie said, waving away his concern. She knew Ryce had been upset at T.C.'s obvious resentment of her. She wanted to assure him it was only natural, considering the circumstances. "Right now T.C. still sees me as the enemy. Remember, *I'm* the one who told him he couldn't come to live with you in the first place. It's only natural for him to feel resentment. In the back of his mind, I'm sure he thinks that I'm just hanging around waiting for you to make a mistake so I can take him away. Once he's feeling secure, he'll come around."

Ryce's eyes held hers for a long moment, and Willie could see a faint shadow reflected in the beautiful blue depths. "Do you think he'll ever feel secure?" Ryce asked quietly.

Willie nodded. She knew that Ryce was especially insightful to T.C.'s feelings. Security was such a fleeting thing. It took years to develop and only seconds to shatter. "I'm sure of it," she told him confidently. "You've just got to give him some time. You know you're good *with* him and good *for* him," she said gently, wanting Ryce to know that she no longer had any reservations about placing T.C. with him.

Ryce looked decidedly uncomfortable at the compliment. "Does this mean you no longer think I'm brash, brazen and pugnacious?" he teased, and Willie laughed. Little by little she was beginning to understand him. He was still brash, still brazen, but it was his own way of self-protection. His way of keeping people at bay. And he was very good at it, she decided. As long as he could keep things light and snappy, no one could get close to him. Ryce had a whole bag of tricks for keeping people at arm's length.

"That depends," she said, cocking her head to look at him. "Do you still think I'm a high-strung, rigid pain in the—"

"Ms. Walker!" Ryce clucked his tongue in admonishment. "Such language. In a house with a child yet." Smiling, Ryce relaxed back on the couch, his hands locked behind his head. "I can't imagine where you ever heard such a thing," he said airily, watching her emotions play along her face. Willie was so beautiful. Open. Honest. So...special.

He'd spent a good deal more time than he should have thinking about Willie. For some reason she was always hovering in his mind. Just thinking about the taste of her, the smell of her, made his blood heat up. His body responded instantly to thoughts of her.

His mouth suddenly turned downward, and Ryce tilted his head, diverting his thoughts. Willie Walker was getting closer to him and the wall he'd built around his heart than he'd ever let anyone get. He really didn't understand how he'd let it happen.

Sighing in confusion, he glanced over at her again. Maybe it was just gratitude. Ryce blinked, and the muscles in his stomach tightened. Hell, what he was feeling for Willie had nothing whatsoever to do with gratitude. No. What he was feeling for Ms. Wilhelmina Walker had nothing to do with gratitude. He pushed the thought and the feeling to the back of his mind.

Watching Ryce, Willie sensed he was about to retreat from her, and she didn't understand why. It was like last night, when he kissed her. She had a feeling that whenever she got too close to seeing the real Ryce, an invisible wall slammed down, shutting her out. But why?

"T.C. seems to have taken a shine to Morty," she said, trying to keep the subject light.

"Can you beat that?" Ryce said with a shake of his head. "The two of them act like they've known each other years instead of hours."

"Ryce," she said carefully, watching his reaction. "Did you know about Morty's son?"

"I know all about him," he said curtly. His face hardened, and she knew it was a subject he didn't want to pursue. His withdrawal was quick and complete this time. But she was willing to let it go, for the moment, adding it to the little file in her head of things to find out about Ryce.

Smiling, Willie pushed herself out of the chair, desperate to get back the light mood they'd shared for most of the day. "Hey, in all the excitement I forgot to give you your present."

"Present?" Ryce sat up, his brows drawn together in a heavy frown of confusion. "You bought a present for me? What for? It's not my birthday."

"I know that," she said simply, knowing she was treading on dangerous ground. The look on his face was as dark as midnight. Buying him a present had been an impulsive act. But it was done now. "Actually, it's for both of us," she clarified mysteriously, enjoying the confusion on his face. "Come on. I'll show you. It's in the kitchen."

Why had she bought him a present, he wondered, following her through the door into the kitchen. He couldn't remember the last time anyone had bought him a present. Ryce came to an abrupt halt, swiveling his head in every direction. "Lord, Willie, this doesn't even look like the same kitchen. You've really done a job in here." He chuckled softly. "Hell, I never knew the counters were that color."

"I didn't do it all. Morty insisted on scrubbing the floor for me. He said it wasn't the kind of work for an elegant lady like me." With a haughty sniff, Willie curtsied formally, playing the light moment for all it was worth. It was so good to see Ryce relaxing and letting down his guard with her.

"He's right, you know." Ryce turned to her, pinning her with his bold, blue gaze. He openly studied her until she felt her blood zip through her veins. "When I asked for your help," he said softly, reaching out to run his finger down her nose, "I didn't expect you to become a scrubwoman."

What he could do to her with just a look of those bold, blue eyes, Willie thought, trying to get her thudding pulse under control.

Ryce's nearness was enough to send her heart soaring. She had to keep her personal feelings under control. If she didn't, Willie knew she was asking for trouble. "Come on," she said, grabbing his elbow and steering him toward the other end of the kitchen. "Let me show you your present." With Ryce in tow, Willie marched to the garbage can. Above it, she'd attached a miniature basketball hoop. Ryce threw back his head and started to laugh.

Willie smiled. What a nice laugh he had, she thought again, feeling warmed all over. Why couldn't he just let go, she wondered sadly. Why couldn't he just trust her enough to let her inside the wall he had around his heart? She had a feeling Ryce didn't even know how much he had to offer someone.

Ryce's blue eyes lifted to caress her gray ones as he fingered the hoop gently. He touched it as if it were the most exquisite gift on earth. The knot he carried around inside of him loosened just a bit. He was touched beyond measure by her thoughtfulness. "You bought that for me, Willie?" he asked, his eyes warming as they gently caressed her weary features.

"Maybe your aim will get better," she teased, remembering all the missed baskets from the morning. "I saw it at the furniture store and knew I had to buy it."

She seemed so happy, standing there looking up at him with those expressive gray eyes. Raw hunger rose up in Ryce. He longed to tell her how much he appreciated her gesture, how much she and her company had meant to him today. But he couldn't.

He'd never been the kind to verbalize his feelings. He'd been too busy running away from them. Oh, if it meant whispering sweet nothings that *meant* nothing to a woman in the middle of the night, well, hell, he could do that. Anybody could. But he had a feeling Willie wasn't like that. She wasn't a woman who would settle for worthless whispers or one-night stands. Willie would want it all. Love, marriage, commitment. The thought, and all the implications that went with it, scared the hell out of him.

Ryce took a deep, lung-filling breath. Willie's hair was a tangled mess, tumbling around her shoulders in a dark halo. Her shirt was spotted, the tails hanging haphazardly around her waist. She smelled of disinfectant, but it was more potent than the most expensive perfume. His body went hard with longing. And it wasn't just physical, he realized, but a whole lot more. His eyes darkened and met hers in the suddenly quiet room.

"Ryce?" Willie's eyes clouded with uncertainty as she laid a hand on his chest. She could feel the rapid thud of his heart beneath his shirt. What was he thinking, she wondered. His face was soft, his eyes warm as they caressed her face. For the first time he looked... open and vulnerable. The bleakness she'd seen so often in his eyes was gone, replaced by a shred of... hope.

"Come here," Ryce ordered huskily, lifting her hand off his chest and tugging her close. "I haven't had a chance to talk to you all day." He wanted to touch her again, to feel her pressed against him, to taste the sweet honey of her lips. *He wanted her.*

Willie didn't have time to reason her actions. She went to him, knowing she wanted nothing more than to feel his closeness. To feel his lips pressed against hers again.

Ryce's gaze dropped to caress her lips. He lifted his hands to anchor her face. His fingers gently stroked her tender skin. Wide-eyed, Willie watched him, wondering what was going on in his mind. Nervously, she licked her suddenly parched lips. Ryce's eyes followed the movement of her tongue, and she shivered.

"Willie?" Her name shuddered out of his lips.

Sweet anticipation ripped through her, weakening her knees. She whimpered softly as his hands slid down to span her waist. Ryce hauled her close, pressing his hard masculine length against her soft feminine frame.

Eagerly, she parted her waiting lips as he fastened his mouth over hers. Her breathing quickened in instant response, and Willie's eyes fluttered closed in rhapsody. Ryce delicately touched her. His fingertips gently brushed the curve of her jaw, the lobe of her ear, the sweet hollow of her neck. She lifted her arms, sliding them across Ryce's wide expanse of shoulders, settling firmly around his neck.

He slid his palm upward to caress her cheek. His rough fingers touched her reverently, breaking down all her defenses. Moaning softly, she pressed closer to him as his mouth moved slowly over hers, possessing her, branding her with his own virile mark.

Her thoughts swirled as she tried desperately to resist the temptation of Ryce. She wanted to kiss him, wanted to feel the sweet pleasure his touch brought to her. But she didn't want him to withdraw from her again. Every time he did, it was like he slammed a door in her face. Why couldn't he open up to her? Why couldn't he trust her?

Overwhelming sensations stormed her body, sending her senses into a spasm of wild pleasure. Ryce slid his hand to her ribcage, gently soothing, caressing. She felt her skin heat up under his touch.

Ryce's breathing became heavy, and she could feel the trembling of his hands on her waist as he pulled her ever closer. Willie arched against him, moaning softly as his kiss deepened, taking her breath with it.

Oh, Ryce, she thought, tightening her arms around him.

Oh, Willie, he thought, pulling her closer still and trying to resist his own private emotional demons.

A shudder tore through Ryce. She felt it seep from his body into hers, searing them together. There was a possessive fierceness in the way Ryce held her. She felt cherished and protected, knowing she shouldn't feel any of those things.

Ryce couldn't give all of himself to anybody, and she knew she would never settle for anything *less* than *all* he had to give.

The thought saddened her, breaking through the fog in her brain. All too soon he would withdraw from her in every way. The thought brought a sudden shaft of pain to her thudding heart. She didn't know if she could stand Ryce's withdrawal. Again. She was in too deep. Somehow, when she wasn't looking, the rude, rough cop had stolen her heart.

The thought brought her up sharply when she realized the depths of her own feelings, feelings that had nothing to do with her professional status. Her eyes slowly fluttered open, and despite the fact that she wanted the moment to go on forever, she had to protect her heart. Ryce was not the kind of man who could give and take love. He didn't want hers or any-

one's. She knew it as sure as she knew her own name.
The thought saddened her deeply, and Willie gently
pulled back from him as the knowledge and depth of
her feelings engulfed her with sadness.

Ryce looked deep into her eyes, perplexed and confused at her withdrawal. He was the one who usually
retreated, not her. A spasm of pain touched his heart.
Is this what she felt every time he retreated, he wondered sadly, feeling suddenly bereft.

If it had been anyone else but Willie, he would have
taken it as rejection. But not Willie. She wasn't re-
jecting him, of that he was sure. She couldn't, not with
the way she responded to him. There was something
magical between them. He'd felt it, and he was certain so had she. So why had she pulled back?

He leaned his forehead against hers and looked deep
into her gray eyes. "What's wrong?" he asked, his
voice shaky. His breathing was quick and shallow as
he tried to control his own reactions.

Willie glanced away, deliberately avoiding his gaze.
She really didn't want to put into words what she was
feeling for him. She was afraid he might read her feelings in her eyes. If he knew just how fast and how far
she'd fallen for him, she knew Ryce would turn tail
and bolt as quickly as his long legs could carry him.
She knew she couldn't afford his withdrawal, not now.
Maybe—just maybe—she might have a chance to
break through all of the barriers he kept around his
trust and his heart. But she would have to move slowly
and carefully.

"It's nothing," she lied, forcing her lips into her
shaky smile, lips that suddenly felt lonely and lost
without his. "It's just that...well...I'm supposed to
maintain a professional relationship with the parents

and the kids. And..." Willie lifted her eyes to his and instantly knew it was a mistake. She was lost.

Ryce slid his arms around her waist, his fingers possessively digging into her soft flesh as he dragged her back to him. "You can be professional after."

Willie blinked. "After... what?"

"After this." He dipped his head and caught her mouth.

Sighing with pleasure, she wound her arms around him again. Weakness was a trait she'd never allowed herself. Until now. With Ryce, she felt weak, vulnerable and totally off base. She'd never had a problem separating her personal life from her professional one before. But then again, she'd never met anyone like Ryce before. She didn't want just part of him. She wanted *all* of him. The good with the bad, *everything* he had to give. For now she would take what he could give and savor it. For now it would be enough. She hoped.

Opening her mouth for him, Willie groaned softly as pleasurable sensations flowed through her. He was right. She could be professional... *after*.

"Hey, Ryce!" T.C. barreled into the kitchen. "Wait until you see what we—" T.C.'s arms were loaded with brown grocery sacks that slid to the floor when he caught sight of Willie and Ryce. They jumped apart quickly, but apparently not quickly enough.

T.C. turned and fled from the room. Ryce muttered a wicked oath, then dragged a hand through his hair.

"I'd better go talk to him," he said, reaching out to touch her cheek. "I'll take care of T.C. Why don't you give Morty a hand?" Willie nodded. Without another word, Ryce strode out of the room.

"I'm sorry, Billie," Morty said softly. He'd followed T.C. into the kitchen. Willie had been so embarrassed at being caught kissing Ryce that she hadn't even noticed he was there.

"It's all right, Morty," she lied, forcing a bright smile. "Here, let me help you with those bags."

By the time Ryce came downstairs again they had all the groceries put away, and Morty had dinner in the oven. Willie watched fascinated as Morty took over the kitchen. He'd refused all offers of help, relegating her to setting the table.

"Something smells good," Ryce commented, coming into the kitchen. Willie's eyes met his, and her breath caught as she waited for some signal from him as to how T.C. was.

"He's fine," Ryce said with a smile, sensing her concern. He reached out to run a finger down her nose. "Willie, look, you're exhausted. Why don't you go stretch out on the couch and let me help Morty."

"Not much left to do, Mikey. It'll be about another hour and a half so... if you don't mind, I think I'll use your facilities to take a hot shower. Timmy and I stopped and picked up a change of clothes for me. If I'm going to be having dinner with you folks, the least I can do is clean up."

"You go right ahead, Morty," Ryce said, without taking his gaze from Willie's. "Willie here is just going to rest until dinner's ready. Aren't you?" His tone of voice left little doubt that the matter had been decided.

"But, I—"

"No buts about it," Ryce said, dropping an arm around her waist and steering her toward the living room. "You've done enough for one day. Curl up on the couch, now. We'll call you when dinner is ready."

"Are you always this bossy?" she inquired testily, as Ryce stood guard over her until she'd curled up on the couch under his watchful eye.

"Always," he confirmed, nodding his head. "Now don't move until I wake you for dinner. I'll be in the kitchen if you need me."

Still scowling, Willie watched his retreating back. *If you need me,* he'd said.

Oh, Ryce, she thought sadly, *you'll never know how much I need you.*

"Willie?" Ryce's sweet breath buffeted her face, and she stretched leisurely.

"Mmmm," she murmured, turning away from the disturbing presence.

Ryce smiled. She looked so soft and sweet all curled up asleep. Not a bit like the woman who just yesterday had come storming into his office, fully intending to do him bodily harm. Yesterday. God, it seemed like a lifetime ago. So much had happened. So many changes. So many feelings. Ryce pushed the disturbing thoughts away and bent to kiss Willie's cheek.

"Willie, dinner's ready. Come on, hon, it's time to get up." He trailed a bouquet of kisses down her cheek and across her neck. Her skin was warm from sleep, and he allowed his lips to find the soft recesses of her neck. He buried his face in her softness, savoring the wonderful scent of her. God, she smelled good. Warm and welcome. He knew he should keep her at arm's length, but looking at her, watching her, he knew he couldn't keep her at bay any more than he could stop breathing. Gently, he reached out and touched her cheek.

"Whoever you are," she murmured without opening her eyes, "be forewarned, I know a rude, rough cop."

"Rude and rough!" He went for her waist, sliding his fingers under her blouse to tickle the sensitive skin. Willie let out a howl of laughter. With arms and legs flying, she knocked Ryce to the floor with her hip as she tried to get away from his rampaging fingers.

"Hot damn, woman," he complained, pulling himself to his feet. "I didn't know you were so ticklish." He rubbed his backside. "Or so dangerous. We could use you on the force."

Willie jumped to her feet, pausing to smooth out her blouse. "Let that be fair warning, Ryce. I'm a lady who can take care of herself."

His eyes met hers, and he smiled as she looped her arm through his. He couldn't remember ever enjoying such a warm camaraderie with a woman before. The only women he knew were the kind whose name he wouldn't remember in the morning. Women who wouldn't take the time to get past all the barriers he put up. He had a feeling Willie wasn't at all like those women. Willie was a woman who played for keeps. The thought coiled his stomach into a tight ball.

"Something smells good," Willie commented, entering the kitchen and taking a seat. The table was filled with fragrant dishes. A roast pork sat majestically in the middle of the table. A plate brimming with stuffing and dumplings accompanied it. Morty looked right at home as he fussed over the food like a mother hen.

"Dig in, now, before it gets cold," Morty instructed, picking up the plate of pork. She didn't know how he did it, but the kitchen was just as clean as it was before he prepared the meal.

Willie took the platter from Morty, and her eyes met T.C.'s. He was sitting sullenly in his chair, glaring at her. Boy, if eyes could talk, Willie thought, amused, T.C.'s would be X-rated. He'll come around in time, she thought hopefully. He'll come around.

"Ryce, do you have plans for that extra bedroom upstairs?" T.C. asked around a mouthful of food.

"Don't talk with your mouth full, Timmy," Morty admonished, tapping T.C. lightly on the wrist.

"Sorry," the boy said sheepishly, hurriedly swallowing his food. "Do you, Ryce?"

Ryce looked over at the boy. "No, not really. Why, did you have something in mind?"

T.C. cast a glance at Morty who nodded his head in encouragement. Ryce and Willie exchanged confused glances. Something was up between the two, that much was clear.

"Well, I was thinking. Morty here doesn't have a place to stay. And he cooks real good. You told me last night you were going to have to get someone to stay with me when you were on duty, so I was wondering..." T.C.'s voice filtered off, and Ryce stopped eating.

"T.C.," Ryce said quietly, setting his fork down on the table and giving the child his undivided attention. "I don't ever want you to be afraid to talk to me about anything. Understand? No matter how bad it is, no matter what the problem, I want to know about it. Got it? I'm always here for you. *Always*. Now, what's up?"

T.C. lifted his eyes to Ryce's. "I . . ." He glanced at Morty. "I—well—I was just wondering. Morty here, well, he needs somewhere to stay, and we need someone to cook for us and look after me when you're on duty. So I was just wondering. Why couldn't Morty move in here with us? We have plenty of room," T.C. went on, his voice picking up excitement. "Morty could stay in the extra bedroom upstairs. That way he'd be here all the time, and you wouldn't have to worry about me when you're on duty, or at school." He glanced at Willie. "And then we wouldn't need *her* help," he said disdainfully. "Anyway, I think it would be great."

Ryce looked at T.C. thoughtfully. For the moment, he was willing to let the insult to Willie slide. He would handle it in a minute. Right now, he wanted to get this matter settled. For T.C. to reach out and trust Morty after such a short time gave him hope. Maybe Willie was right. Maybe eventually the child would feel secure. He sure as hell hoped so.

"I think that's a great idea," Ryce said. "But we'd have to find out how Morty feels about it. You know, T.C., we can't just go rearranging the man's life for him without even asking what his plans are."

All eyes turned to Morty, who dropped his gaze and pushed his food around with his fork. "Well, Mikey, to tell you the truth, me and Timmy here, we already talked it over. But I told him it was up to you. I kind of like the idea of settling in." He glanced at Ryce seriously. "And you don't have to worry," he said quietly, "I'll stay off the sauce. Ain't got no need, now." He glanced at T.C. affectionately. T.C. looked at Ryce, and Ryce looked at Willie.

Willie knew Ryce was waiting for her opinion. Morty was no longer just a street person to her, but a real person with feelings and emotions. The affection he had for Ryce and T.C. was genuine. In his own way, Ryce was helping not only T.C., but Morty as well. Funny, but now they all had someone to care about and a reason to care. They all had someone else in their lives, they all belonged to someone. She glanced at Ryce.

"T.C.," she began, sensing it was an opportunity to mend some fences with the child. "I think that's a wonderful idea."

T.C. ignored her, turning his attention back to Ryce. "What do *you* think, Ryce?" T.C. asked, clearly making it known that Willie's opinion didn't matter one whit. She felt a twinge of hurt but banked it down. She had to give the child time, she reminded herself.

"It's fine with me," Ryce said, smiling at T.C. and Morty. "We can move your stuff in tomorrow."

"All right!" T.C. cried, jumping up from the table. "Why can't we do it tonight? Morty says he don't have much. After dinner we can get his stuff from the shelter. That way he can stay here tonight. There's an old movie on TV that Morty says we've got to watch. Right, Morty."

"Right," Morty agreed, pulling out T.C.'s chair and indicating T.C. was to get back in it. "But no movie for you until you sit down and finish your dinner. After the dishes are done and the kitchen's cleaned up, then we'll see about moving me in. Now eat."

"After dinner, I'm going to take Willie home," Ryce said with a smile, watching as T.C. wolfed down his food. "So I'd better get you a spare key, Morty." Getting to his feet, Ryce pushed through the swinging

door and grabbed the spare house key he kept in the
living room.

Ryce turned to go back into the kitchen. He stopped
just short of the doorway. Darkness had fallen. Willie had turned on one of the new lamps, and the house
was bathed in a warm, rosy glow. Long golden shad-
ows played along the wall. Ryce glanced around the
familiar room as if seeing it for the first time. Something was different. Absently, he fingered the key in
his hand as his eyes scanned the room again. In just a
few days, Willie's presence had made a difference, not
only in his house, but in his life.

Morty and T.C.'s voices intermingled with Willie's
soft laughter floating into the silent room. For the first
time since he bought the house it didn't reek of loneliness. Ryce smiled slowly as an unbearable weight
lifted from his heart. It sounded like ... *home*.

Chapter Seven

"T.C.," Morty scolded, "you're not going anywhere until you finish your eggs."

"But Ryce is waiting for me," T.C. complained. "We're going to be late for the game."

"The game can wait. Ryce and Billie can go on ahead without us. We'll follow along when you're done," Morty insisted, dropping a restraining hand on T.C.'s shoulder and flashing a wink at Ryce. "You finish your breakfast, now."

"I think that's a great idea," Ryce said, downing the last of his coffee and jumping from his chair. "Come on, Willie, let's go." He grabbed her hand and literally pulled her from her chair.

"Ryce," she protested, struggling to keep up with him as he tugged her along and out the door. "What on earth is the hurry? The game doesn't start for a half an hour. Why are you in such a hur—"

"Get in," he ordered, bundling her into his car.

"The man's crazy," she muttered crabbily, watching as Ryce rounded the car and hopped in. "Would you please tell me what is the matter with you?" she demanded, wondering why a moment ago she was leisurely enjoying a cup of Morty's coffee, and the next thing she knew Ryce was dragging her out of the house like a smelly cat.

"Nothing," he said, clearly not intending to elaborate further as he started the car and tore away from the curb. Frowning, Willie watched as he drove a block and then abruptly pulled over to the curb and killed the engine.

"Ryce! I demand to know—" His lips descended on hers, silencing her. His mouth was hot and fierce as it claimed hers. Willie's eyes fluttered closed, and she leaned into him, deciding to question his behavior later.

"God, Willie," he whispered, teasing her mouth with his own and feeling the hunger build within him. "I've missed you," he murmured, pulling her close until she was pressed tightly against him. He nuzzled her ear, his mouth gently stoking the fire growing within her.

"Missed me?" she croaked, trying to control the erratic beating of her heart. "We've spent nearly every single day together for the past three weeks."

"Yes," he muttered, tracing a trail of heat from the sensitive lobe of her ear down the gentle curve of her neck with his lips. "But we haven't had five minutes alone."

It was true. T.C. hadn't given them five minutes alone since the day they'd bought Ryce's furniture and Morty had moved in. The past three weeks had been wonderful, though. She'd spent nearly every non-working moment with Ryce and T.C.

Morty had moved in and seemed to meld right into the scheme of things. T.C. and Morty were like two peas in a pod. The relationship between the old man and the young boy was wonderful to watch. As was the relationship between T.C. and Ryce.

Since T.C. had entered his life, Ryce seemed to have mellowed. He'd let his guard down. He no longer seemed quite so hard and cold. He laughed more, and occasionally Willie caught him looking at her with a gentleness that took her breath away. More than once over the past few weeks, she was certain she'd finally broken through the wall of Ryce's heart. But still, she wasn't sure. She still wanted to tread carefully.

Ryce and Morty had welcomed her into their makeshift family, including her in everything from Sunday brunch to Saturday night at the movies. T.C., on the other hand, was quite a different story.

He still had a great deal of resentment toward her, and she really didn't know why. Willie had thought that in time his animosity would soften. But, if anything, it seemed to be getting worse.

She'd worked with children most of her life, and it was rare when she couldn't get through to one. But she hadn't made any headway with T.C. His treatment of her bordered on downright rudeness. Ryce had tried to crack down on T.C., but Willie knew no amount of ordering could make the child like her. T.C. was careful now.

When Ryce was around, T.C. all but ignored her. When Ryce wasn't around, T.C. made sure his feelings for her were clear. On more than one occasion, Willie had thought of talking to Ryce about it, but she decided against it. Ryce had been trying so hard to be a good parent, he'd done everything she could have expected. He had done so much in order to conform to the rules and regulations, and to make a good, suitable home for T.C., that she didn't have the heart to tell him about T.C.'s obvious hostility toward her.

The child made it his personal responsibility to see to it that she and Ryce were never alone. It was as if he was deliberately trying to keep them apart. And he was succeeding.

These few stolen moments alone with Ryce were heaven, Willie thought, lifting her mouth hungrily for his kiss. A contented sigh slipped through her lips as she melted against Ryce, allowing herself the pleasure of him.

His fingertips feathered gently down her neck as his mouth worked over hers. He pressed his tongue gently against the seam of her lips, and her body tightened, humming in sensual response.

Moaning softly, she willingly parted her lips, welcoming the warmth of him. A sunburst of sensations exploded inside her, and she shivered, sliding her arms tighter around Ryce and allowing her fingers to tunnel through the silky depths of his hair, drawing him even closer.

Ryce's breathing grew ragged as he gently caressed Willie. He couldn't get enough of her. He wanted her in ways he never thought possible to want someone. Slowly, he slid his fingertips across the softness of her shoulders in a feather-light caress. His body tightened and grew hard as he ran his hands slowly up and down her sides, caressing her ribs with his thumb.

A low moan escaped her as Ryce gently cupped her breast, nestling her against the warmth of his palm.

Willie's mind spun wildly as he caressed her. His warmth mingled with hers. Her breath rasped in the early morning air as her body tightened against his hand, filling her with an ache of fire and need.

His mouth ground into hers, taking and possessing her. He could feel the rapid beat of her heart against his hand. Her labored breathing matched his own, ragged with pleasure. He moved his hands slowly, gently over her breasts. Billows of pleasure rolled over her, and Willie shivered despite the warmth of the day.

Ryce, I love you, she thought, pressing her mouth closer to his.

Willie, I love you, he thought, accepting the treasure she offered.

The thought hit him with the force of a blow, and Ryce dragged his lips from hers. The walls around his heart slammed shut. He couldn't love her. He couldn't love anyone. Loving made him vulnerable.

Ryce pressed her head against his shoulder and rested his face against her cheek, trying to stop the floodgate of emotions tearing through him. Willie sensed he'd withdrawn from her, and it saddened her. Would she ever get used to it, she wondered, feeling the anguish of pain constrict her heart.

Ryce ached with loneliness. He wanted to brand the moment in his heart and his memory forever. He knew that no matter how he tried to deny it, he loved Willie. Loved her as he'd never loved anyone. But he couldn't put into words what was in his heart.

Fear rose up and overtook him. Loving meant trusting, trusting meant giving up control. It meant letting go and giving someone the power to hurt him. He didn't know if he could do it. He didn't know if he even wanted to try. He loved Willie, but he wasn't sure it was enough. Trust. Love. They were foreign and frightening to him.

"Ryce?" Her voice was soft and laced with pain. Instinctively he tightened his arms around her. "Why?" It was only one word, but it spoke volumes. "Why do you close yourself off to me? Whenever I think I'm about to get close to you, you withdraw. Why?" She had to know. She loved him so, she wanted him to learn to trust her, and then maybe someday, he would even learn to love her.

He turned his head and dragged a hand through his hair. "I don't know," he said honestly. "I just don't know."

"Do you think you could learn to trust me?" she asked, biting her lip to keep the tears from falling. How could she get through to him? What would it take to break through the wall of pain and hurt he'd enveloped himself in?

"No—yes." He shook his head. "I don't know, Willie. All I know is that when I'm with you I feel..." His voice trailed off, and he looked at her, his eyes bleak. Why couldn't he put into words what was in his heart? He saw the tears sparkling in her eyes, and he swore softly. "Don't cry," he said, lifting a finger to wipe her lashes. He never wanted to hurt her. He wanted to love, cherish and protect her. But he didn't even know if he could. "Willie, I don't know if I'll ever be able to..." He looked at her sadly.

A spark of hope fanned her heart, and Willie lifted a hand to stroke his cheek. "It's all right," she whispered, knowing she would just have to give him more time and be patient. "We'll just take each day as it comes."

"I'll try," he promised, flashing her a sad, lop-sided grin. Their eyes met for what seemed an eternity. "I'll try, Willie." He pressed a quick, hot kiss to her mouth, wanting to let the subject drop. "We'd better get going. This is the last game of the season, and our team only needs one more win to make the regional finals." Reluctantly, Ryce unwound his arms from her and started the car.

Willie glanced up at him as he drove. What a beautiful profile, she thought, laying her hand on his warm, strong thigh. He glanced at her quickly, a wicked smile on his lips.

"Willie, honey," Ryce said with a laugh, "if you don't move your hand, baseball is going to be the *last* thing on my mind."

"He was *safe!*" Willie yelled, jumping to her feet. "Are you blind?" she cried, whipping Ryce's cap off her head and waving it in the direction of the harassed umpire. "Someone get the ump some glasses! The man's blind as a bat!"

"Billie, Billie," Morty admonished, grabbing her arm to restrain her. "Calm yourself, honey."

"But Ryce was safe," she protested, ignoring the other spectators in the stands watching her display with growing interest.

"I know, honey," Morty chuckled. "But remember what happened last week?"

"Are you saying it was my fault I got thrown out of the park?" she demanded, her temper in full bloom as she remembered the humiliating scene.

Morty's eyes twinkled. "No, honey. I'm not saying it was your fault. You're entitled to say whatever you want. But I don't think insulting the umps is going to help Ryce's team. You've already been warned twice. I'd hate to see you have to go sit in the car for the rest of the game again this week."

Willie scowled dejectedly. Ryce's rudeness was rubbing off on her, she thought humorously. Never in her life had she ever exhibited such a wanton display of bad manners. But how was she supposed to know that the umpire had the right to banish not only the players from the game, but the spectators as well? She'd been mortified last Sunday when—after a one-sided verbal battle—the umpire had mounted the bleachers, whipped off his cap, pressed his wrinkled face into hers and yelled, "You're out!"

"But Ryce was safe," she insisted, settling Ryce's cap back atop her head and frowning at Morty.

"Willie," T.C. muttered, deliberately pretending like he'd never seen her before in his life, "will you sit down and shut up."

"Timmy!" Morty's voice was sharp, but Willie put a restraining hand on his arm.

"Don't, Morty," she said quietly, determined to handle this problem herself. "T.C.," she began carefully, sinking down into her seat and directing her attention to the angry child, "why don't you tell me what the problem is?"

"*You're* the problem," he grumbled, doing his best to ignore her.

"And why am I the problem?" she inquired, struggling to keep her temper in check. Professional or no professional, she'd had just about enough of T.C.'s smart tongue and insolent behavior.

"Because," he said evasively.

She reached out and turned his chin toward her, forcing him to look at her. His eyes burned with anger and hatred. For a moment, Willie almost backed down.

"Why don't you tell me what you've got against me, T.C.?" she said gently, determined to find out just what was wrong with the child and why he obviously hated her so much.

"Nothing," he muttered, pulling free of her grasp and glaring at her. "I'm just sick of you always hanging around."

Willie worked to cover her hurt feelings. T.C. was deliberately being cruel, deliberately trying to insult and hurt her. It wasn't the first time a child had taken his resentment and his fears out on her. But this was the first time it was a child she was personally involved with, a child she truly cared about, and it hurt.

"Is that what you think I'm doing?" she inquired softly, working hard to keep her voice neutral. "Hanging around?"

"Isn't it?" he challenged.

"T.C., I am in charge of you and your welfare. It's my job to see that you've been placed in a proper home. Ryce asked me to help him make sure that both him and the house conform to the rules and regulations set forth by the state. That's all I've been doing." It wasn't quite what she wanted to say. She wanted to reach out to the child, to touch him and tell him how much she'd come to care about him. But she sensed he wouldn't allow it. In some ways Ryce and T.C. were the same. They'd closed themselves off from love for so long that they no longer knew how to give or accept it.

"We don't need your help," T.C. snapped, "so why don't you just shove off?" He stood up abruptly and sauntered down the stairs.

She stared after his retreating back. She knew that T.C. felt resentful toward her, but why such hatred? She didn't understand it. Willie sighed a deep, pain-filled sigh. It was just another hurdle for her to over-come. She would have no future with Ryce—that is if she could ever get over the emotional barriers *he* kept up—without breaking through and abolishing T.C.'s hate. It was going to be a challenge, she decided.

"I'm sorry, Billie," Morty said gently. "He don't mean no harm."

"I know," she said sadly, dragging up a smile. "I just don't understand why he hates me so."

"Ah, honey, he doesn't hate you. You gotta under-stand a kid like T.C. He's been alone for a long time. He still thinks of you as the enemy. He probably fig-ures you're hanging around just waiting to take him away from Ryce. He'll come around, wait and see. Once he sees that you're not a threat, well, I reckon he'll soften up a bit."

"Maybe," Willie said less than confidently.

"I'm sure of it."

"And what if he doesn't, Morty?" She shook her head, wondering why T.C. was the one child she couldn't seem to get to. She considered it a personal as well as a professional challenge. Not only for the child's sake, but for Ryce's as well. "I don't under-stand, Morty. I really don't. He seems to have taken right to you. He treats you like a long lost... grandfather. Me, he treats like a communicable disease."

Morty chuckled softly, shaking his gray head. "Did you ever think maybe you're trying too hard?"

Willie's eyes widened as she turned to look at him. "What do you mean?"

"Well..." Morty scratched his chin. "This brings to mind when my Timmy was a boy. His mamma died, and a few years later I fell in love with a woman. A good woman, mind you, but that didn't matter to my Timmy. He saw her as a threat to his mother's memory. Gracie—well—she tried real hard with Timmy, but the more she tried, the more resentful he became. Finally one day she just got tired of trying. Before you knew it, that boy was hankering around her like a lost pup. He realized that he'd lost something special. Gracie was a real special woman. When he saw how happy she made me, well, he came around. You mark my words, once T.C. realizes how much Mikey cares about you, I'm sure the boy will see that you aren't a threat. He'll see that you make Mikey happy, and sooner or later he'll come around."

She looked at him curiously. "Morty, what makes you think Ryce cares about me?"

Morty flashed her a grizzled smile. "Honey, I may be old, but I ain't blind. Any fool can see Mikey cares about you. I told you once before, Mikey's a loner, but that don't mean he ain't got feelings. He hasn't had an easy time of it, I guess. He don't talk much about it, but I got a sense about these things. It may take him a while to admit it, but he cares about you, I know." Morty glanced off into the distance, and Willie's heart warmed. If only what Morty said was true. If only she knew for sure that Ryce cared about her.

"You know, honey," Morty said, giving her hand a gentle squeeze. "You've sure brought a lot of happiness to all of our lives. You're a very special lady. Even if that dang kid doesn't realize it, yet."

"Oh, Morty," she breathed, leaning over to kiss his cheek. "Thank you. You're pretty special yourself."

Flustered, Morty stood up. "Look, the game's over. Here comes Mikey. I'd better go find T.C. I think it might be best if him and I walk home. I think he needs some time alone. We'll meet you back at the house."

"Morty?" She placed a hand on his arm. "Thank you."

He grinned. "You're welcome, Billie. Keep your chin up," he instructed, smiling as he went down the stairs.

"Hey, Willie!" Ryce called, bounding up the steps toward her with a happy smile. "We won." He bent to kiss her, his eyes twinkling wickedly. "Even though the umpire was blind as a bat!" He flashed her that heartbreaking grin of his. "Come on, let's go. I'm starved. Morty promised me a celebration dinner if we won. I've invited Sal Giordiano to dinner. You don't mind, do you?" he asked worriedly, and Willie laughed.

"Mind?" She followed Ryce down the bleacher steps. "How could I mind, Ryce? I don't even know what a Sal Giordiano is."

"Not a *what*, Willie," Ryce teased, bumping against her hip. "It's a who, Willie. A *who*. Best damn cop I ever met. He was my first partner. Taught me everything I know. He's working robbery now. Or at least he will be when he goes back to work." Ryce suddenly grew grim.

"What's wrong? What do you mean when he goes back to work?" Her heart began to pound. She knew police work was dangerous, but it was something she tried not to think about.

"He's on leave right now." Ryce dropped his arm around her shoulder and guided her toward the car. "Where's Morty and T.C.?" he asked, looking around worriedly and clearly trying to change the subject.

"They went on along without us," she said, climbing into the car. "Now tell me about Sal," she prompted, unwilling to let the matter drop.

"Can't get anything past you, can I?" he asked with a smile, as he climbed behind the wheel. "About six months ago Sal and his partner were on a stakeout. There was a mix-up in signals, and Sal's partner was killed."

"What happened?" she inquired, moving over closer to Ryce as he placed a hand on her shoulder and nudged her closer.

"I don't know. Sal won't talk about it. Not even to me. All I know is that there was an investigation, and he's been on 'leave' pending the outcome of the investigation." Ryce started the car and drove out of the parking lot.

"He's a good friend, isn't he?" Willie inquired with sudden interest. In all the time she'd known Ryce, she had never met any of his friends. Sal must be someone pretty special. And the fact that Ryce had invited him to dinner was another indication that Ryce was perhaps learning to open up to her, to share a part of his life with her.

"A very good friend. He's been staying at my cabin at the lake for the past few weeks. He came down today to play in the game, so I invited him to dinner. He needs a friend right now, Willie," Ryce said somberly, and Willie's heart warmed. Ryce always seemed to be helping someone. T.C., Morty and now his friend Sal. He had so much to give to someone. Would he ever be able to give all those things to her? Would he ever want to? She could only hope.

Ryce pulled into the driveway and turned off the engine. "Speaking of the cabin, Willie, I've been thinking. T.C. starts school next week, and I'd like to go up there for a few days. What do you say?"

She frowned. "I don't see any problem in taking T.C. to the cabin. It's not like you're taking him out of the state and I know where you're going."

Ryce smiled wryly and scratched his brow. "Uh, Willie, that's not exactly what I mean. I was wondering if you'd like to come along. Now before you say anything, Morty will be there to chaperone, and there's three separate bedrooms. The swimming's great, and the fishing is even better. So...what do you think?" There was a plea and a promise in the depths of his blue eyes, and Willie felt a warmth of tenderness scamper over her. She smiled into his uncertain face.

"I'd say we'd better go inside and have dinner. I've got to call Fergie and tell her I won't be in for a few days. Then I've got to pack."

He angled his head toward her. "Hot damn, Willie!" he said with a grin. "Hot damn!"

Chapter Eight

I'll say one thing for you, Ryce," Sal Giordiano said, wiping his mouth with a napkin. "Your taste in cooks *and* women has improved remarkably. Now if we could just do something about your disposition." Flashing Willie a wink, Sal pushed himself from the table. Over six feet tall, with a thick head of curly black hair, deep olive complexion and dark, almost black eyes, Sal was an extremely handsome man. He had a lazy, knock-em-dead smile and an easy-going personality. Sal was relaxed, and totally at ease with himself and the world around him, in direct contrast to Ryce, who was always in control. Sal and Ryce were total opposites. Yet, despite their differences, it was easy to see that the two men were good friends. Although she'd been a bit nervous about meeting him, Sal had immediately put Willie at ease with his affable charm. She'd liked him immediately. There seemed to be a masculine camaraderie between Ryce and Sal

that was delightful to watch. Ryce seemed more at ease
with Sal than Willie had ever seen him before.

"Listen, Giordiano," Ryce grumbled, pushing his
plate away and rolling to his feet. "You leave my cook,
my woman, and my disposition alone. I'm doing just
fine without your help." Ryce dropped a protective
hand on Willie's shoulder and smiled down at her.

My woman. Willie's heart tumbled over in surprise. She wondered if Ryce realized what he'd said.
Sal flashed her a secret smile of silent understanding.
He knows, she thought silently. *Sal knows I'm in love
with Ryce.*

"All of you, scat!" Morty ordered with an indis-
criminate wave of his hand. "Out of my kitchen—not
you, T.C.," he said pointedly. "*You* get to stay and
help with the dishes."

"Why do I always get stuck doing the dishes?" T.C.
wondered, glaring at Willie. "That's *woman's* work."

"Woman's work!" Willie cried in exasperation,
unwilling to let that particular insult slide by. She'd
had just about enough of T.C.'s insults and rudeness. Being professional was one thing, being a fool
for an eleven-year-old child was quite another matter.

"T.C., there's no such thing as *woman's* work,"
Ryce insisted, jumping into the fray before it esca-
lated. "Come on, kid, *I'll* help with the dishes. That
is, if I can trust Sal here with Willie." He cast a du-
bious eye on his former partner.

"Trust me?" Sal inquired, theatrically placing a
hand on his heart. "Why, Ryce, you've wounded me
to the quick. You know I am the absolute soul of dis-
cretion."

"Yeah," Ryce grunted, as he began to clear the table. "Then why do they call you Smooth, Suave Sal?"

"Come on, dear lady," Sal said, gallantly helping Willie from the chair, "let me take you away from all this."

"Willie, don't you believe any of his cops-and-robbers stories," Ryce called. "That man's got a line as long as a rap sheet."

Laughing, Willie followed Sal into the living room. She curled up on the couch, tucking her feet under her, while Sal chose the chair. For a long moment, Sal didn't say anything. He just sat there looking at her. Finally, he grinned broadly.

"What?" she asked in confusion, wondering what all the staring and smiling was about.

Sal chuckled softly. "I never thought I'd see the day Ryce would be tamed by a woman. But you've apparently got that guy tied up in knots." He flashed her a boyish grin. "It's nice, Willie. Ryce is a great guy. Not too pleasant at times, but one hell of a guy."

"I know, but what makes you think I've tamed him?" she inquired curiously, feeling intensely pleased by his words.

"Now come on, Willie, I'm a cop, remember? I've known Ryce a hell of a long time. I've never known him to spend more than one evening in the company of a woman." Sal cleared his throat. "And you aren't...uh...exactly the kind of woman Ryce generally spends his evenings with." Grinning, Sal leaned forward and motioned toward the kitchen, indicating that he wanted Ryce to hear him. "Ryce is used to the kind of woman who—"

"I heard that, Giordiano," Ryce called from the kitchen. "Keep it up and I'll tell Willie the story about how you lost your car, your gun and your pants—"

"Never mind," Sal called, his face growing red. "I won't say another word. My lips are sealed."

"Keep it up, and that ain't all that's going to be sealed," Ryce warned, poking his head through the door. "Willie, don't believe anything he tells you."

"Go clean the kitchen," Sal ordered, waving Ryce away. Sal turned his attention back to Willie, who was thoroughly enjoying the bantering between the two men. It was the first time she'd seen Ryce totally open with anyone. It was a wonderful sight to see.

"You know, Willie," Sal said seriously, "I knew right away you must be someone special. I could tell just the way he looks at you. Ryce's eyes never left you all through dinner. He followed your every movement. I'd say he's hooked, all right." Sal grinned, and Willie's heart soared.

"Well," she admitted shyly, "I'd say I'm hooked on him, too." She looked at Sal carefully, deciding instantly to trust him. "Sal, do you think..." Her voice trailed off as she suffered a twinge of doubt.

"What?" Sal prompted gently. "Come on, Willie. I know Ryce probably better than anyone. Anything you want to know, I'm the guy to ask."

"Sal, do you think—well—do you think it's possible for Ryce to ever trust anyone?" she asked hopefully, wearing her heart on her sleeve and not really caring. "I mean, do you think he'll ever be able to open up and let someone in his life and..."

"And into his heart?" Sal finished for her, and Willie nodded solemnly. He looked thoughtful for a moment. "Willie, let me tell you how it is with him.

Ryce is *not* an easy guy to know. Or to love," he added deliberately. "But he's the kind of guy who is in there for the long haul, know what I mean?" She nodded, and Sal went on. "Listen, Willie," Sal encouraged, sliding forward in his chair, "you hang in there. I promise you, it will be worth it. There's not many guys I'd trust with my life, but Ryce is one of them. If he's your friend, he's your friend for life. I've got a feeling he's going to feel the same way about a woman. And I've got a hunch *you're* that woman. You're just going to have to be patient."

Patient? She could be patient for as long as it took, as long as there was hope.

"Do you think you can do that?" he asked, and she nodded. There was a long moment of silence, as if Sal was giving her time to deliberate his question.

"So... what do you think about T.C.?" she asked finally, breaking the silence.

"I think he's a brat," Sal said with a laugh. "It's just like Ryce to take in that kid. But Ryce and T.C. are perfectly suited. I think Ryce will be good for him. And *you're* good for Ryce. I like you, Willie. Just don't hurt him." His voice had dropped an octave, and Willie read the thinly veiled threat in his words. "He's a good man and a damn good cop. He's not easy to get to know, but well worth the effort."

"I know, Sal," she said with a smile. "And I have no intention of hurting him."

"Good." Sal grinned, his eyes twinkling with wicked mischief. "Did I ever tell you about the time Ryce—"

"That's enough, Giordiano," Ryce said, coming into the room. He had a dish towel draped across his shoulder and a wide smile on his face. He plopped down on the sofa right next to Willie, dropping a hand possessively on her leg. "Now you know why they call him Smooth, Suave Sal," Ryce said knowingly, wiggling his brows at her suggestively.

Willie laughed, happy to see Ryce in such a light, playful mood. Sal was right. Ryce *was* worth every effort. She laid her hand over his, and their eyes met for a long, silent moment. Her heart filled with joy. Oh, how she loved him.

"I can tell when I'm not wanted," Sal grumbled, looking affectionately at their entangled hands. He pulled himself from the chair. "I better shove off, Ryce. I'm back on duty tomorrow."

Ryce stood up, looking surprised. "How's the investigation going?"

"It's over, thank God," Sal said soberly, running a hand through his dark curls. "I just want to put it behind me and get back to work. Listen, Willie, it's been nice meeting you." He crossed the room and gave her a peck on the cheek, under Ryce's watchful eye. "And you," he said, playfully poking Ryce in the stomach, "thanks for the use of the cabin. Say goodbye to the kid for me. I'll talk to you soon."

"Well, what did you think of him?" Ryce asked once Sal had left.

Willie had a feeling it was important to him how she felt about Sal. "He's very nice," she said. "Is he married?"

"Sal?" Ryce laughed and shook his head, dropping his hand over hers again. "No. He—"

"Ryce?" T.C. came into the living room, looking more sullen than nine days of rain. "The kitchen's all done." His eyes zeroed in on their entwined hands, and his face grew darker.

"Come on in and sit down, T.C. There's something I want to ask you."

"What?" T.C. flopped into the chair Sal had vacated, resting his head in his hand.

"School starts next week—now stop groaning T.C.—I told you you're going to school, like it or not. It's the law, right, Willie?" He looked at her for encouragement, and she nodded.

"T.C., in order for Ryce's adoption of you to go through, we have to prove to the state that he's conformed to all the rules and regulations set forth for foster parents. And," she added, smiling, "that includes school."

She could have saved her breath. If T.C. heard her, he gave no indication. He deliberately averted his gaze to stare at the floor. *Sal is right,* she thought testily, *the kid is a brat.*

She immediately felt remorseful. It wasn't T.C.'s fault for his behavior. Life had dealt him a rotten hand, and she was just going to have to be more patient. It was just that T.C.'s behavior was getting to her. She made a mental note to be more patient with him. If only for Ryce's sake.

"Anyway," Ryce went on. "I've got a cabin down in Southern Illinois. I was wondering if you'd like to go down for a few days and maybe do some hunting and fishing?"

T.C. jumped from the chair, his eyes dancing with excitement. "You mean it, Ryce? I've never been hunting. Can Morty go with us? Oh boy, wait until I tell him." T.C. turned and bolted toward the door.

"Willie's coming, too," Ryce added, and T.C. stopped abruptly. He turned to them, looking thoroughly dejected.

"Oh." A look of hurt darkened T.C.'s eyes.

"Go on, go tell Morty," Ryce instructed, trying to bridge the gap of the awkward moment. "We're leaving in the morning, right after sunrise, so you better get packed and to bed." Nodding and muttering under his breath, T.C. shuffled off to tell Morty.

"I'd say I was about as welcome as a flea at a dog circus," Willie said moodily, feeling hurt despite her efforts to feel otherwise.

"He'll come around. At least that's what one very smart lady once told me." Ryce glanced at her. "You've got that look on your face, again, Ms. Walker."

"What look?"

"The fire-and-brimstone-rules-and-regulations look," Ryce said, pulling her around so that she was lying across his lap. "Something on your mind?" he inquired, looking at her intently. "Have I violated one of the procedures or something?" he asked, his eyes darkening as they settled on her moist lips.

Willie shook her head. "No. Of course not. I'm just a bit worried about T.C. Do you think he's going to give you a problem about going to school?"

"No."

She glanced up at him in surprise. "No? Just like that?"

His jaw hardened. "Just like that," Ryce said firmly, leaving little doubt that as far as he was concerned the subject was closed. "Remember, Willie, I told you no kid of mine is going to run wild. T.C.'s going to toe the line and do what he's told, and that includes going to school. If he doesn't like it, that's tough. It's nonnegotiable. He's too young to realize how important an education is, but I'm not. Besides,

I'm not about to let anything jeopardize his adoption. And if it means he has to do some things he doesn't like, well tough shi—turkeys. Everyone has to do some things they don't like. Hell, nobody said life was fair."

"Speaking of school, Ryce, you never told me what *you're* going to school for."

"I know." He dipped his head, gently teasing the soft crevices of her neck with his tongue.

"Ryce . . ." Willie gasped as the familiar feelings of longing whispered across her nerve endings. His touch never failed to ignite a wave of desire and longing. But it wasn't enough. She wanted so much more from him. After seeing Ryce with Sal, after seeing the easy, open way he behaved with his friend, she knew without a doubt that Ryce was capable of giving more. What would it take to make him that open with her.

"Ryce," she murmured huskily, snuggling closer to him. "You didn't answer me."

"Didn't I," he whispered, trailing his mouth up and down her neck, teasing the tip of her earlobe with his tongue until shivers of desire rolled over her.

"N-no, you didn't," Willie finally managed to get out, pushing him away and sitting up. "Now, *tell me*," she ordered in her best fire-and-brimstone voice.

A lazy grin slid across his features, causing her heart to tumble over. "I'd rather do what we were doing," he whispered, reaching for her again. Shaking her head, Willie leaned out of his reach. "All right," he said in resignation, settling for wrapping his arms around her and pulling her close. "It's no big deal, Willie. I'm going to school to finish my degree."

"What degree?" she asked in confusion, trying to keep her mind on the conversation and not on the sweet flow of warmth that was seeping into her veins from his touch and his nearness.

"My law degree," he said softly, tilting her chin up to capture her lips with his. Her eyes fluttered closed for a moment, until his words penetrated her foggy brain.

"Law degree!" she cried, yanking her lips free of his. Rude, rough, unorthodox Ryce was going to be a lawyer! "Why didn't you tell me?" she demanded, thumping his chest.

A lopsided grin tilted the corners of his lips. "You never asked," he growled, leaning forward to tease the corners of her mouth with his tongue. "Besides," he murmured, planting soft, feathery kisses on her eager mouth, "I don't recall my educational background being part of the interrogation for adoption. It's not, is it?" he asked, pulling back to look at her with some concern.

"No, Ryce, it's not," she said, laughing at the look on his face. "*You*, a lawyer?" she said again, shaking her head. "I can't believe it."

"Well, you don't have to act like I said I was going to start wearing dresses or something," Ryce complained, clearly looking affronted.

"No. No. No," she said, wanting to reassure him. "It's wonderful. I'm just surprised. What made you decide to be a lawyer?" she asked, settling herself more comfortably in his arms.

He tightened his arms around her, resting his chin on the top of her head. "Well, I figured that if I can't change the damn system being a cop, maybe I can go back to where the system starts and change things that way. I figured it's worth a try."

She smiled. For a man who proclaimed not to care, Ryce cared very much, about a lot of things. It only softened her heart more toward him.

"Ryce?"

"What?" he murmured, burying his face in her hair and inhaling deeply.

"You're not so tough," she teased.

"I'm not?" he grumbled. "Well, don't ever repeat that. Think what it will do to my reputation."

"Ryce?"

He sighed. "Now what, Willie?"

She grinned mischievously. "How did Sal lose his car, his gun and his pants?"

Ryce sat up abruptly. "Oh, no," he said, shaking his head and trying to banish a wicked grin. "That's one story you're not going to get out of me. At least, not tonight. Come on, I'd better get you home. We're leaving at sunrise, and you need your beauty sleep." He stood up and drew her into his arms. His eyes searched her face, and she smiled up at him. His arms tightened around her, and he held her close. "Not that you're not beautiful now." His eyes locked on hers, and he took a deep breath. "Willie?"

"What?" She leaned her head against his shoulder, savoring the masculine scent of him.

"I think ... I think ..." Ryce swallowed hard, forcing himself to say the words he felt so deep in his heart. "I think you're ... pretty special."

She lifted her head. She knew how difficult it was for him to verbalize his feelings, and her heart soared. While it was hardly a declaration of love, it would do—for now. "I think you're pretty special, too, *Michael*," Willie whispered, lifting her head to look at him.

"You've never called me Michael before," he said quietly.

"You've never said I was special before," she retorted, unwilling to let him retreat from her this time.

"You are, you know. *Very* special," he said somberly, and her heart filled with love for him.

"Michael . . ." Willie swallowed hard, wondering if she should put into words what she was feeling in her heart. Did she dare? What if he backed off from her? What if she scared him off completely? She wanted to take the chance. She loved him so. "I—I—"

"Morty and I are going to bed," T.C. said, bursting into the room without preamble. Scowling at Willie, who was still wrapped in Ryce's arms, T.C. stomped through the room and up the stairs. "I thought *she* was going home," he grumbled.

"*She* is going home," Willie snapped, furious because T.C. had not only ruined the moment but her disposition as well.

Ryce sighed and dropped his arms. "That kid! I'm sorry, Willie. I promise I'll have a talk with him. You'll see. He'll be different in the morning."

"No," Willie said, shaking her head. "Leave him be, Ryce. He'll come around. *Eventually,*" she muttered, allowing Ryce to walk her to the door. She didn't want Ryce interceding on her behalf. She didn't want T.C. to have something else to hold against her. If he felt Ryce was taking her side over his, that's exactly what would happen.

"I'll pick you up at sunrise," Ryce said, giving her a quick, hard kiss.

Nodding, Willie walked to her car. While they were at the cabin, she was going to have her own little talk with T.C. Like Ryce said, it was time T.C. learned how to behave around civilized people. And she was just the person to teach him!

Chapter Nine

Ryce?" Willie murmured, turning over on her tummy and adjusting herself more comfortably on the lawn chair. "Are you asleep?"

"Mmmm," came the muffled response.

Smiling, she propped herself on her elbow to study him. He hadn't moved in almost an hour. He'd just lain there, soaking up the sun, the warmth and the glorious summer day. Dressed in skimpy black swimming trunks and nothing else, his long, lean body was stretched out comfortably on the lawn chair. The lazy days in the sun had burnished his body to a deep copper color, making him even more attractive. "I thought you said we were going to have a picnic." she complained good-naturedly.

"Have we got sun?" he murmured without opening his eyes.

Willie glanced up at the sun-drenched morning sky. "We've got sun," she assured him, basking in the warmth.

"Have we got fresh air?"

She inhaled deeply, savoring the clean, country air. "We've got fresh air."

"Have we got food?" Ryce murmured, lifting his arm over his head, and settling deeper into the chair.

She glanced at the picnic basket sitting between them on the pier. Morty had prepared their luncheon feast before taking T.C. out on the lake to fish. He'd packed enough food for a month-long siege. "We've definitely got food," she said with a laugh.

"So..." Ryce murmured hazily. "We've got sun, fresh air and food. Seems to me we've got a picnic."

"Want to go for a swim?" she asked, getting up and perching on the edge of his chair. She trailed her fingers slowly down the thick mat of dark hair on his chest.

"Do I look like a man who wants to go for a swim?" he grumbled, squirming as her fingers made contact with a sensitive area.

"Are you ticklish?" she asked with a wicked smile.

One bold blue eye opened. A hint of mischief danced in his gaze. "Watch it, lady," he warned, a lazy smile curving his lips. "I know a rude, rough cop who doesn't take kindly to meandering fingers." He grabbed her arms and tumbled her down next to him so that they were lying side by side, their bodies stuck together from the suntan oil.

"What are you doing?" she asked cautiously, squirming slightly from the heat of his body, which had nothing whatsoever to do with the sun.

His grin widened. "My favorite thing."

"And that is?" she inquired with a raised brow, feeling the heat of his gaze as it slowly traveled over every inch of her.

"Looking at you." Threading his fingers through her hair, he tipped her head back and looked at her. He smiled slowly, and her pulse quickened. "Did I ever tell you you're beautiful?"

"No," she stammered, her voice a bit breathy.

"Well, lady," he drawled, sliding his fingers slowly up and down her arm, "you are." His fingers lazily traced a pattern on her bare shoulder, causing a streak of heat to ripple over her body.

"Thank you," she murmured, flustered at the unexpected compliment. Ryce was letting go—just a bit—little by little every day. A fanning flame of hope was born in her heart.

Since they'd arrived at the cabin three days ago, they'd spent almost every waking moment together. It had been the happiest three days of her life. They had done everything together. And nothing. It didn't matter what they did, as long as they were together.

"It's getting warmer," she murmured, feeling flustered as his fingers did a teasing dance on her bare skin. She turned to glance at the serene, crystal-blue lake. The gentle lapping of the water against the pier had a soothing, hypnotic effect.

"Could get a lot warmer," he murmured, dipping his head to kiss her shoulder. "You taste good, suntan oil and all."

She shifted, trying to adjust herself so she wasn't leaning into him so much. She could feel every solid square inch of him, and once again she thought how perfectly they fit together.

Ryce seemed so much more relaxed up here, she thought hazily, letting the rhythm of his fingers lull her into a sensuous fog. Calmer, too, much more at peace with himself. Ryce had dropped the hard, arrogant facade. In fact, he'd been warm and playful since they arrived. She'd seen a different side of him, a warm, caring side that only reinforced her feelings for him. Hope flared anew that she was making some progress. Perhaps he would learn to open up, to let go, to love her. Perhaps.

Ryce sighed wistfully, planting a soft bouquet of kisses across her cheek. "Tomorrow we'll go home. You have to go back to work. T.C. will be starting school, and in a few more weeks, my vacation will be over, too." Ryce sighed languidly. "I hate to see the summer end."

She laughed softly. "You make it sound like it's the end of a lot more than summer." Didn't he know it was just the beginning?

"Willie?" he murmured, nibbling gently on her shoulder. His warm breath heated her bare skin. "Have I told you how much I appreciate all you've done for me and T.C.?"

She laid her head next to his and looked into his eyes. Eyes that were no longer bleak and empty, but soft and sincere.

"No, you haven't," she whispered; their lips were only a breath apart. Unable to resist temptation, Willie leaned forward and gently brushed hers across his in a feather-light kiss.

Ryce groaned softly, adjusting his body closer to hers. "Well, I do—appreciate everything you've done," he rasped, leaning his mouth closer. His breath mingled with hers, and he slid his arms around her, drawing her close to his masculine heat. Arching against him, Willie felt her breath come out in raspy little jerks. "If it wasn't for you," he murmured, kissing the sensitive corners of her mouth, "I wouldn't have T.C." His mouth closed over hers, and he drew the very breath from her lungs.

Willie slid her hands up his powerful arms, straining now with the effort of holding her. She kissed him back. Her lips were pliant and willing under his. He flicked his tongue over her moist lips, a low, growling sound escaping from deep in his throat.

Her body grew limp and heavy as the tip of his tongue did butterfly strokes against her own. Her eyes closed tightly in ecstasy. His hands incited her, roaming slowly to knead the bare flesh of her shoulder, the slope of her arm, the curve of her breast. His touch gentled as he stroked her breast, and Willie sighed, shaking in the wake of her own desire for him. She moaned softly as he cupped her breast in his palm, the heat searing through the warmth of her suit.

"Willie." Her name rasped out of his mouth against hers. "I—I—" He tried to tell her how he felt. He wanted her to know how much he cared for her.

"Ryce?" Her lids fluttered open at the tone of his voice, and her heart stilled, waiting for the words she longed to hear. Her breath caught in anticipation, waiting, wondering what he was trying to say. Her eyes met his in sun-drenched passion.

He wanted to tell her—to let her know how she'd stalked his thoughts and haunted his dreams. But he couldn't. His hands stilled, and he gently cradled her against him, breathing deeply, slowly, trying to control himself. Stunned and perplexed by the depth of his feelings for her, Ryce pushed them away, suddenly scared.

"What, Ryce?" she whispered, laying her head against his shoulder and looking up at him wistfully. "What were you going to say?" *Please open your heart and let me and my love in,* she pleaded silently.

"It was nothing." His mouth snapped shut, and he flung himself back against the chair, throwing an arm over his face to stop the haunting thoughts. He wanted to tell her, but he just couldn't. "I just wanted you to know how much I appreciate all you've done. If it wasn't for you, I wouldn't have T.C. It's been almost a month, and I think things are working out very well."

Hurt by his dismissal, Willie sat up. "I didn't do anything. You did it all. All I did was set out the rules and regulations. You're the one who followed them. I think you've done an admirable job with him. He's really coming around. I don't think there will be any problem with his adoption."

"Thank you," he said curtly.

How could he lie there and calmly tell her how much he *appreciated* her? She didn't want to be appreciated, she wanted to be loved. Her eyes traveled over his wonderful face, and disappointment etched the caverns of her soul. She wanted his love. Nothing else would do. Not now. Not ever.

Ryce could feel her tensing beside him. He had thought he could say it. He had thought he could verbalize what was burning inside of him for her. His thoughts and feelings kept him awake at night and tortured by day. He wanted to express them. He wanted her to know he . . . loved her.

But he couldn't. He just couldn't. To admit his feelings was to leave himself vulnerable. To do so was to give someone control over him, the ability to hurt him. He couldn't—no, wouldn't—do it. Long ago he'd closed off his emotions to everyone. He couldn't let go. Not now. Not yet. Not even for Willie.

He glanced at her, huddled miserably on the chair. He saw the pain in her face, in her eyes, and he felt anguished. He had caused that look. He had caused that pain. He wanted to reach out to her, comfort her, erase the pain in her eyes, but he couldn't. Too many memories, too much hurt. He didn't know if he would ever be able to do it.

"Still want to go for a swim?" he asked softly, wanting only to erase the pain on her face.

Willie deliberately avoided his eyes and shook her head. "No, thanks. I think I'll just lie here for a while." She got up and reclaimed her own chair. Lying down, she closed her eyes tightly, trying to stop the stinging tears from falling.

She heard him rise and walk down the pier. Unable to resist, she opened her eyes and watched him soar off the edge in one graceful flowing movement. He hit the water with barely a splash.

A hot, silent tear slid down her cheek. *Ryce, I love you.*

"Hey, Willie, I've got a present for you," T.C. cried, running up the pier toward her. "Look what I picked up for you!"

"Oh, God," Willie groaned, seeing the worm. She rolled over on her back, and did her best to ignore T.C., who was standing directly over her.

"You're blocking the sun," she grumbled. "It's a bit difficult to get a tan with no sun, T.C.," she said through clenched teeth, desperately trying to hold on to her temper. She'd been in a foul mood ever since this morning. After Ryce had taken his swim, he'd waited for Morty and T.C. to come back with the boat, and then he'd gone out on the lake to do some fishing. She hadn't seen him in several hours, but it was just as well. It had been the first time in three days they'd been apart, and she needed some time to think and sort out her feelings.

"T.C., if you're through showing me your—" she searched for a polite word "—present, would you please move?"

"I was just trying to be pleasant," he insisted, grinning unabashedly and thoroughly enjoying her look of disgust.

"Do you have a dictionary?" she inquired sweetly, squinting up at him.

He looked momentarily confused. "A dictionary? No. Why?"

She lifted her head. "Because I strongly suggest you look up the word 'pleasant.' I guarantee you it has no resemblance to your behavior these past few weeks."

"Yeah, well, those are the breaks," he quipped before belly flopping into the icy-cool lake and sending a riveting spray of cold water over her sun-drenched skin. Willie screeched.

"I'll give you *breaks*," she grumbled, sitting up and grabbing a towel to dry herself off. Muttering under her breath, Willie lay down again and closed her eyes.

They were going home in the morning, and she needed some time to think, to put her feelings in perspective. Never a quitter, she'd even toyed with the

idea of just letting go, letting Ryce and his closed off
heart become a distant memory. But she knew she
couldn't.

She loved Ryce, and she couldn't give up on him.
Not now. She was just going to have to hang in there
and wait. Sal had told her to be patient. But how long
was she going to have to wait? It didn't matter, she realized sadly. She would wait for Ryce forever, even if
it took the rest of her life. She had no choice. She was
hopelessly in love with him.

Ryce couldn't or wouldn't verbalize his feelings. She
could only pray that he *felt* something for her. While
he hadn't put his feelings into words, his smiles didn't
lie, nor did the reverent look in his eyes. Love flared
anew in her heart, filling her with a precious shred of
hope. Ryce had come so far, if only... She sighed
heavily.

T.C., on the other hand, was another matter, she
thought, lifting her head to watch him flop around in
the water. Despite her good intentions to have a talk
with him, there really hadn't been the time. He'd been
so involved with Morty for the past three days that she
hadn't seen him for longer than five minutes. Which,
now, seemed like a blessing. He was surly and downright rude to her, and she'd just about had it with the
kid.

Never in her life had she thought that she would give
up on a child. But she was about to give up on T.C.
What was with him, she wondered. Why did he hate
her so?

It was such a shame, Willie thought sadly, sitting up
as T.C. began to swim laps. He really wasn't a bad kid.
He'd grown and changed since coming to live with

Ryce. Aside from his treatment of her, T.C. was just like any other eleven-year-old kid.

Once again she was glad she had agreed to let Ryce have custody of the boy. Ryce was a wonderful parent. Caring, devoted, loving, yet firm. He'd done everything that was required of a foster parent without complaint. She had no doubt he would make a wonderful *permanent* parent. T.C. couldn't get away with anything. Ryce knew his every move before T.C. made it. Except where she was concerned.

Her gaze wandered back to T.C., who was busily and deliberately splashing her with water. *He's probably hoping to drown me,* she thought dismally, swiping at the beads of water pooled on her legs.

It wasn't enough that she couldn't get through to Ryce, but even if—by some miracle—she did break through the walls he'd built up, how on earth did she ever expect to have a relationship—a permanent relationship—with him when T.C. hated her? Every time she thought about T.C., her hope died a little bit. She knew how much he meant to Ryce. Ryce adored the child. How could they have any kind of relationship when T.C. detested her? Willie sighed deeply. She had to get through to T.C. first, and then she would concentrate on Ryce.

It was ironic really. For years she'd counseled foster and adoptive parents about patience and love when handling a new child in the family. And now she, with all her experience, couldn't handle one young boy. Was she fighting a losing battle, she wondered.

Willie lay back down on the blanket, lost in thought. She'd tried everything she could think of to win T.C. over. Maybe Morty was right. Maybe she'd been trying too hard.

She heard T.C. pull himself up onto the pier. A moment later she felt a blast of ice-cold water as he shook himself like a shaggy dog right over her.

That did it! Willie jerked to a sitting position. "You think you're pretty funny, don't you?" she accused, anger clipping her words.

"Me?" T.C. said with feigned innocence. "I'm not laughing, am I?" he asked, snatching the towel she had lying on the bottom of her chair. He briskly dried his hair, then slid the towel over his soaked body before dropping it in a soggy heap on her lap.

Willie picked up the towel and threw it right back at him. "I've had just about enough of your rudeness, T.C. Why don't you just tell me what the problem is?"

"Problem? I already told you. *You're* the problem." He flopped down on the chair next to hers and, displaying an exaggerated yawn, did his best to ignore her.

Willie was not deterred. "And why am I the problem?" she persisted, unwilling to let the matter drop. She wanted this settled once and for all, for both their sakes.

He shrugged noncommittally, then turned his back to her. Willie counted to ten, then let out her breath slowly. She was *not* going to lose her temper. Well, she amended, it was a little too late for that.

"T.C., how can you ever expect us to get along if you won't tell me what's bothering you?"

"That's just the point, Willie," he said, dragging her name out like some kind of social disease. "I don't *expect* us to get along."

"And why not?"

"Why should I?"

"Because," Willie said, softening her tone, "I care very much about you and about Ryce. I think he cares about me, too. It's getting very difficult for me—for us—because of the way you treat me. Ryce is very aware of the tension between us. It bothers him just as much as it bothers me. I haven't allowed him to say anything to you because I wanted to handle this my own way." Willie took a deep breath. "T.C., if you're worried that I'm hanging around just waiting for Ryce to make a mistake so I can take you away from him, you're wrong. I know at first I was against the idea of Ryce getting custody of you, but I was wrong. Very wrong. I think Ryce is the best thing that ever happened to you. He's the perfect parent. In fact, I'm going to make a recommendation that he be allowed to apply for formal adoption. Then nothing or no one can ever take you away from him."

She'd tried to reassure him, tried to let him know in her own way that she cared for him, too. What would it take to get through to him?

T.C. lifted his head and glared at her. "You know, you're dumber than I thought."

"W-what do you mean?" she asked.

"You really think Ryce *cares* about you?" T.C. shook his head and laughed. "You really *are* dumb. The only reason Ryce has kept you hanging around is to make sure he got custody of me."

Willie shrank back from his words. She blinked as tears burned her eyes and a numbing uneasiness stole over her body. "What makes you say that?" Her heart and mind refused to believe the child's vicious words. It wasn't possible, was it?

"Look, Willie, I'm going to give it to you straight. Face it, you're no great shakes in the looks department. What makes you think a guy like Ryce would be interested in someone like you? Nah, he don't care about you. Ryce ain't no dummy. He knew that to get me he'd have to get past you. He probably figured if he kept you around, paid some attention, maybe you'd change your mind about him." T.C. grinned suddenly. "It worked, didn't it? Hey, once the adoption gets rolling, you'll be gone faster than snake eyes at a crap game."

Willie suddenly went still. Her eyes burned and her lungs hurt from the effort of breathing. Had Ryce deliberately set out to use her?

Oh God! All this time she believed that Ryce cared about her. But she was wrong. All he cared about was using her to get what he wanted. Remembering Ryce's words, she realized the truth of T.C.'s statements.

All I have to do is get past you. I'll do anything to get custody of T.C.

Ryce's words echoed in the tunnels of her mind, squeezing her heart in anguish.

Slowly, Willie forced her shaky legs to move, and she stood up. Hurt and betrayal burned her soul. She loved Ryce, totally and thoroughly, and he used her, lied to her. That was the reason he never said "I love you." He simply didn't. He was stringing her along until she filled out the papers necessary to ensure his custody of T.C.

She grabbed her cover-up, sunglasses and oil, rapidly throwing them into her bag without seeing or caring. Her legs nearly buckled beneath her. She had to get away. She had to run from the pain that was searing her heart. But Willie knew there was nowhere to run, nowhere to hide. The pain was there and always would be. Clutching the wet towel, Willie forced her legs to move. Her body was rocked by the force of pain echoing through every inch of her body. She blinked against the suddenly harsh sunlight and felt the world begin to fade.

"Hey, T.C., Billie, it's time for dinner," Morty called, walking down the pier toward them. "Billie?" Morty saw her paleness, the trembling of her hands. He came closer, carefully examining her face. "What's wrong, honey? What's happened?"

She raised stricken eyes to his. "Nothing," she whispered, her voice cracking. Pushing past him, she ran down the pier and up the path to the cabin. Once inside Willie hurried to her room and shut the door. Silently, she wept, letting the hot, salty tears fall down her cheeks. Now she knew why she couldn't break through to Ryce, why he couldn't let go and trust her. Love her.

Love her. The words reverberated in her mind, taunting her. *Love.* She'd been so blind. How could she love him so much and not have that love returned even just a little? But she knew Ryce didn't love her. Ryce couldn't love anyone, not and use them the way he'd used her.

Willie threw herself across the bed and sobbed until there were no tears left. Morty knocked on the door several times, but she didn't answer. She just lay drowning in her own misery.

Darkness had fallen; the temperature had dropped. Shivering, Willie pulled herself up and began packing. Tomorrow she would try to pick up the pieces of her life and go on, never again to make the mistake of mixing her professional life with her personal one. It had been a mistake she'd paid dearly for. . . . But, she realized, sitting up, it was a mistake that wasn't too late to correct.

Willie finally crept out of her room after midnight. She was exhausted and spent from the hours of tears she'd shed. She stopped abruptly when she saw Ryce sitting at the kitchen table drinking a cup of coffee. He stood up abruptly when he saw her.

"Willie? What's wrong? Morty said you came in before dinner, and have been in your room ever since." He tilted her chin and looked at her red-rimmed eyes. "I've been worried. Have you been crying?" he demanded, twisting her chin gently for a better look. His heart began to pound at the thought. He had hurt her this morning; he'd known it then. But the reality of that hurt reflected in her tear-filled eyes now tore him apart.

She managed a tremulous smile. "No," she lied, moving out of his grasp. "Just resting. All the fresh air and sunshine has really gotten to me. I'm beat." Anxious to get out from under the scrutiny of his eyes, Willie crossed the kitchen and poured herself a cup of coffee. "I'm glad you're here, Ryce. I want to talk to you."

He sat back down and watched as she hesitantly took a seat across from him. "Good, Willie. Because I want to talk to you, too." He slid his hands up and down the coffee cup nervously. He'd spent all afternoon out on the boat, thinking. He could no longer deny he loved Willie, loved her like he'd never loved anyone else. She was warm, caring; she was wonderful. The most caring person he'd ever known. The image of the pain in her eyes this morning when he'd told her he *appreciated* her had haunted him all day.

Hell, he didn't just *appreciate* her. He *loved* her. For
the first time in his life he was ready to admit it. He
was willing to let go of the tight rein of control he had
on his emotions and let someone into his life. And that
someone was Willie.

He loved her, plain and simple. For too long he'd
been alone and lonely, wallowing in the fears and hurts
that should have been banished years ago. He'd
hoarded his emotions in that tiny space inside for so
long that he almost didn't recognize something good
and wonderful when it came along.

Willie. He glanced at her, feeling warmed just by her
presence. She was like a flash of light in his dull,
gloomy life. Hell, he hadn't been living, just existing.
He'd been hiding behind the walls of hurt and despair
that seemed to grow stronger year by year.

It was time to stop hiding, time to take a chance.
He'd wrestled with his emotions all afternoon. Wres-
tled with the demons that had driven him for so long.
But no more, he'd decided this afternoon. *No more.*

He'd been running scared from himself, from Willie, from his own feelings. But he wasn't going to run
any longer.

He wanted something more than an empty life. He
wanted Willie. He thought he would be scared, letting go after all these years, but he only felt a sense of
mounting peace that had eluded him for so long. His
heart no longer seemed frozen, but warm and welcoming. Regrets and caution were thrown to the wind
as the backpack of pain he'd carried for so long dis-
solved into just a fading memory.

For years he had gone along, day by day, never
knowing just what he'd been missing. Willie taught
him all the things he'd never allowed himself to feel

before. Maybe he didn't know all the pretty words of
love, but he would learn. She would teach him. His
frozen heart seemed to open and warm at the prospect.

"Willie?"

"Ryce?" They spoke at the same time, and he
smiled, reaching out to tenderly brush a strand of hair
from her cheek.

"Go on," he urged. "You go first." He could wait,
he'd waited this long, a few more minutes surely
couldn't matter. She was worth waiting for. He'd
waited his whole life for her.

Willie swallowed hard around the lump in her
throat. It was difficult to sit here and try to make polite conversation with him when she loved him so. But
she knew that love would never be returned. She had
to make a clean break of things, free herself from the
ties that bound her to him.

"Ryce," she began slowly, "tomorrow when we get
home, I'm going to turn your case over to another social worker."

Stunned, Ryce's eyes narrowed, and he drew back
as if she'd slapped him. *Case?* "What the hell are you
talking about?" he demanded in confusion.

"Well, I don't think I'm very objective about the
situation. It's seems I've done the unpardonable and
let my personal feelings interfere with my professional judgment." She dared to glance at him. His eyes
were hooded and his face hard. A vein in his temple
throbbed ominously. She had to hurry and get this
over with or she wouldn't be able to do it at all. "I
think it would be best for all concerned if I just turn
your case over to someone else to handle. Under the
circumstances I think it's the only fair thing to do.

Don't worry," she assured him, noticing the darkening expression on his face, "my recommendations will be favorable. I don't think you'll have any problem getting permanent custody of T.C."

Ryce stared at her. Fear, raw and ragged, ripped his soul as the walls of his heart came crashing down. He slammed his cup down, sending the coffee sloshing onto the table. He never knew he could hurt this much. Never knew that one fire-and-brimstone-go-by-the-book social worker had the ability to tear his heart and his life into shreds.

He laughed harshly, bitterly, staring off into the distance. Here he'd been ready to let go, to offer her the world, *his* world. A dark scowl furrowed his brows, and his stomach coiled into a tight little ball that made breathing nearly impossible. He should have run from her when he had the chance. He should have pushed her away and kept pushing until he'd exorcised her from his heart and his soul. But he didn't. Hadn't he learned? He had no home. He didn't belong, not to Willie, not to anyone.

"Is that all I am to you, Willie? A case?" His tone was laced with bitterness, and Willie ducked her head so he wouldn't see her tears.

He was so much more to her, so much more. But she wouldn't be a fool for him or anyone else, ever again. "You have to admit," she said a bit shakily, "I've become personally involved in this case. I—"

"Will you stop using that damn word," Ryce shouted, bolting out of the chair and sending it toppling backward. Her head jerked up in surprise. His eyes were bleak . . . hard . . . empty.

Her heart ached for him, for her. He would never know how much she loved him or what he'd thrown away.

"Ryce, I told you I'd give you a favorable review. You don't have to worr—"

"Yeah, right? I've got nothing to worry about. Get packed," he said curtly. "We're leaving first thing in the morning." Turning, Ryce swore softly and slammed out of the cabin, leaving Willie alone with her pain and her memories.

The ride home was silent and unending. T.C. sat in the front with Ryce. Willie was happy to relinquish the spot to him. She wasn't certain she could sit that close to Ryce, be that near to him, and not try to reach out to him just one more time. But it was no use, she realized that last night. No one could reach Ryce. Not her, not anyone.

Morty sat in the back with her. From the concerned look on his face, Willie knew Morty was aware that something had happened between her and Ryce. He was quiet, though. All the way home he simply held her hand, patting it occasionally in a soothing gesture.

Ryce dropped her off at her apartment without a word. She tried to thank him, but he cut her off. He ordered T.C. to help her with her bags, and the child— to her surprise—did so willingly, without a word of complaint. He was probably so grateful to get rid of her he would have done anything to expedite the process.

As Ryce drove away, fresh, hot tears slid slowly down her cheeks as Willie said a final, silent farewell. *Oh, Ryce.*

Chapter Ten

Would the pain ever stop, Ryce wondered, pushing his food around his plate. Two weeks. It had been two lousy weeks since Willie had walked out of his life. He thought he knew all about pain and loneliness, but in the past two weeks he'd learned all over again. And it hurt like hell.

He thought he was strong, thought he'd protected himself and his heart from the ragged fear and pain. But he hadn't. All it took was one beautiful slip of a woman to tear his heart in two, to bring back all the fear and rejection. He had always been alone, but he'd never felt lonely. Until now. When Willie walked out of his life, she took all the light, all the warmth, all the love.

All the love, Ryce. All the love.

She'd left him in his darkness. Alone and lonely. It wasn't fair.

Who ever said life was fair?

Oh, Willie.

What had he done, T.C. wondered, watching Ryce push his food around his plate for the umpteenth night. He thought it was going to be great, just him and Ryce. But ever since they'd come back from the cabin, ever since he'd told Willie all those lies, Ryce hadn't been the same. He was quiet, too quiet. It was...scary. Sometimes at night he heard Ryce prowling around the empty house. Empty. That's what the house was like without Willie. And so was Ryce. T.C. wanted things back the way they were. He wanted Ryce laughing and happy.

What had he done?

"Uh, Ryce," T.C. said hesitantly, lowering his gaze to his plate, "do you think I could talk to you? After dinner, I mean?"

Ryce pushed his plate away and tried to smile. "Sure, son, whatever. I'm going to sit out on the porch. You finish your dinner and come on out."

"I'm done," T.C. said quickly, following Ryce's lead and standing up. "This is kind of important."

"Well, come on, then." With one arm around his shoulder, Ryce led T.C. out onto the porch. They sat on the steps, the same steps where he'd sat with Willie so long ago. Ryce's heart constricted with pain once again. "What's up, T.C.?" he asked, trying without success to banish the memories.

"I...uh...I wanted to talk to you." Avoiding his gaze, T.C. glumly dropped his chin.

Ryce could tell T.C. was nervous by the way he was fidgeting. "Out with it," he said gently. "Whatever it is, it can't be that bad."

"Yes, it is, Ryce," T.C. whispered, his voice shaky with tears. "I did something terrible."

Ryce dropped an arm around T.C.'s shoulders. "T.C.," he began slowly, his voice low and soothing, "I told you, there isn't anything you can't tell me. There's nothing I won't understand. Why don't you tell me what the problem is?"

"It's Willie," T.C. said softly, lifting his stricken eyes to Ryce.

"Willie?" Ryce frowned in confusion. "What's Willie got to do with this?"

"You're going to hate me," T.C. said glumly, one silent tear rolling down his cheek.

"T.C., I'm not going to hate you. I could never hate you. Now what about Willie?"

"I...I...I kind of lied to her when we were up at the cabin. That last day, before we came home."

"What do you mean you lied?" Ryce asked, his eyes narrowing in confusion. "T.C., what are you talking about? Why don't you start at the beginning and tell me what this is all about?"

"I'm sorry, Ryce," he whispered, his voice cracking as huge tears filled his eyes. "I'm sorry." Sobbing, T.C. flung himself at Ryce, burying his face against him.

Ryce's arms automatically went around the child in comfort. "Sshhh, T.C.," he soothed, stroking the back of the boy's head. "It's all right. Just tell me what you're sorry about."

T.C. lifted his tear-streaked face. "I told Willie that...that...you were only letting her hang around so that you could get custody of me. I...I...lied," he sobbed, his voice cracking. T.C. again buried his face against Ryce's shirt. "I'm sorry. I was just so... scared," he whimpered.

"Scared?" Ryce repeated in confusion. "Of what?"

T.C. lifted his face, and Ryce's heart constricted at the raw fear in the child's eyes. "I ain't ever had anybody love me before. I thought when I came to live with you—well—I thought—that maybe someday you'd love me. But then, when I saw that—that you— were starting to love Willie, I was afraid that if you loved *her*, you wouldn't have any love left for me." T.C.'s eyes filled with fresh tears. "I just wanted you... to love me."

Oh, God. Ryce's heart went crashing against his ribcage. Why hadn't he seen it? Why hadn't he known? He knew what T.C. was going through. Wanting someone's love so badly you would do anything—anything to get it. *Oh, God*. His heart broke for T.C. For himself. He'd been so blind, to Willie and to T.C.

Ryce hauled the sobbing child onto his lap, wrapping him in his arms as another round of sobs shook the boy's slender body. Ryce swallowed hard as a burning pain stung his eyes. So little, so scared, and so much pain. Would it ever go away, he wondered, tightening his arms around his son. Ryce swallowed hard. He would make the fear go away. Just like Willie... his thoughts fragmented. Just like Willie had done. She'd made *his* fear go away.

Willie. Oh, God. No wonder she'd told him all that stuff, no wonder she'd turned her back on him. He glanced down at T.C. The child had wrapped his arms tightly around Ryce's neck. He would deal with T.C. first, and then... He held the child close until his sobs subsided, gently stroking and soothing him.

"T.C.," Ryce finally said. "I...I..." He swallowed hard, no longer afraid. "I love you. *I've always loved you.* Why do you think I wanted to adopt you? I wanted you to know that you belonged here, with me. You'll always belong with me, and no matter what you've done, no matter how wrong it is, I'll never stop loving you. Do you understand?"

T.C. swiped at his eyes and nodded hesitantly.

"Son," Ryce went on. "Love isn't something you use up like...like...a tissue. The more love you give, the more you *have* to give. That's the best thing about love, T.C. No matter how many people you love, there's always enough left inside to love a little more. There's nothing in this world that would make me stop loving you. *I love you,*" Ryce said slowly, saying the words he'd never allowed himself to say or feel before. "I love you, T.C. You have to believe that."

T.C. wiped his eyes. "Do you love Willie?" he asked hesitantly, and Ryce smiled sadly.

"Yes, T.C., I love Willie, too. But that doesn't mean I won't or can't love you. I love you both."

T.C. nodded his head slowly. "I think Willie loves you, too. Things just ain't the same without her. It just doesn't seem the same."

"I know," Ryce admitted sadly, feeling the pain acutely in his heart.

T.C. lifted his head and wiped his eyes. There was a crooked smile on his lips. "I think...I think...maybe we need her, Ryce."

Ryce sighed heavily. "I think you just might be right, T.C."

"We can't let her loose without us. Who knows how many umpires she'll insult. Do you think she'll come back?'' T.C. asked, looking scared and a bit lost again, and Ryce smiled.

"I don't know. But I'm sure as hell going to find out."

"Can I come?" T.C. asked hopefully, climbing off Ryce's lap.

Ryce shook his head. "Not this time, son," he said, getting to his feet. "This is something I've got to do myself."

"Ryce?"

"What, T.C.?"

"Would you tell Willie something for me?"

"Sure."

"Tell her I'm sorry, and . . . I love her."

Ryce smiled, and the floodgates of his heart opened. The kid was learning. What had Willie said? Security took years to develop but only moments to shatter? Maybe now T.C. might feel some of that security. And maybe now, so would he. "How about if you tell her yourself?"

T.C. nodded as Ryce yanked open the screen door and grabbed his jacket out of the closet.

"You go on inside and help Morty with the dishes. There's something I've got to do." Ryce headed down the steps and around the house toward his bike. His spirit was light, his heart soaring. He finally knew where he was going. He was going . . . home.

"You can't go in there," Fergie cried, causing Willie's head to snap up from the papers she was working on. What on earth was all the commotion, she wondered, wearily rubbing her eyes. She was supposed to be concentrating on these forms. Concentrating. A wan smile lifted her lips. She hadn't been able to concentrate on anything but her broken heart for the past two weeks. Not since she'd walked out of Ryce's life.

She kept waiting, hoping. Her hope was fading now, but it still didn't prevent her from turning her head every time she heard a motorcycle or saw a dark head of hair. She heard Ryce's voice everywhere. In her dreams, in her thoughts. Like now. She cocked her ear toward her closed office door. If she didn't know better, she would swear there was the low hum of a motorcycle in the outer office. And she would swear it was Ryce's low growl filtering through the door. But she knew better.

"I said, you can't go in there," Fergie cried again, as Willie's office door burst open. Fergie threw herself into the doorway, blocking the entrance. "You can't go in there!" she insisted.

"I can," Ryce said with a smile, sliding off his bike. "And I will."

"I'm going to call the police," Fergie threatened, and Ryce's grin slid wider.

"Honey," he drawled, lifting her around the waist and out of his way. "I *am* the police." He pecked the astonished clerk on the cheek as he swept past her.

Willie's eyes widened. It wasn't her imagination. It was Ryce's voice. *And* his motorcycle! Slowly she rose to her feet. Only Ryce would be crazy enough to drive a motorcycle into her office. The man was still brash, brazen and pugnacious, but those were definitely not his only good points. God, how she loved him. How she missed him. He looked wonderful, and her heart ached with longing.

"Are you out of your mind?" Willie inquired, and Ryce grinned.

"If I remember correctly, a few weeks back you told me I didn't have a mind, remember?" He stood stock-still, letting his eyes drink her in. No one had ever looked so lovely to him. His heart filled with joy.

Nervously, she fidgeted with the papers on her desk. "What... what are you doing here?"

He slowly walked across the room toward her, a lazy grin firmly in place. His bold blue eyes holding her captive. "Actually, Ms. Walker, I'm here on official business." At that, her hopes began to fall.

"What kind of business?" she asked, hoping her voice didn't betray the ache in her heart.

"I've come to arrest you."

Her eyes widened as he came closer. "You what?" Willie's temper flared. It wasn't enough that the man had used her, betrayed her and broken her heart, now he was going to add insult to injury and arrest her. Oh, no, he wasn't!

"On what charges?" she demanded.

"I believe the charge is *stealing*."

"What?" she cried, incredulous, and Ryce grinned at the outrage on her face. She stiffened her back and glared at him. "Detective Ryce, I'll have you know I have never stolen a thing in my life. And for you to march in here—no, correction—drive in here and accuse me—"

"You're mad," he said unnecessarily, clucking his tongue as he rounded her desk, coming closer, until he was standing toe-to-toe with her. "You know, I never knew you had such a terrible temper. I guess we'll have to do something about that."

"What are you doing here?" she asked, refusing to let her hopes rise. She'd done it too many times. He'd closed her off too many times, and she couldn't take the risk, not again, despite the fact that she loved him with all her heart. Love was no good if it was only one sided.

"I already told you. I came to arrest you." He looked down at her, and there was an unfamiliar light in his blue eyes. Willie blinked in confusion.

"Would you mind telling me just what it is that I was supposed to have stolen?" Her heart was pounding so loudly, she wanted to throw her arms around him and hold on for dear life, but she couldn't. He had to learn to give and take, to share himself, his life. And his love.

"My heart, Willie," he said softly, lifting a hand to gently touch her cheek. "You've stolen my heart." His eyes met hers. "I love you, Willie. Oh, God," he whispered, hauling her tighter against him. "I thought I'd never see you again. Thought I'd never be able to know your warmth, your light. I was so scared." He buried his face in her hair and inhaled deeply. Willie clung to him, letting the feel of him seep into her, loving him.

Oh, Ryce.

He tilted her head up and hungrily covered her mouth. He hadn't felt right in two weeks. Hadn't felt the happiness, hadn't felt the peace. His lips moved against hers, soaking up her tenderness.

Tears filled her eyes. "Oh, Michael," she whispered.

With a low growl, he hauled her closer, covering her mouth with his again. "I've missed you," he murmured between kisses. "I've missed you so much." He tightened his arms around her, pressing her close. "I love you, Willie. *I love you.*" He planted kisses frantically over her face, barely stopping to take a breath.

Now that he'd found her again, he would never, ever let her go. She was everything to him. *Everything.* Sweet satisfaction rippled over him as an inner contentment seeped through his body.

"I love you, too, Michael."

"Will you marry me?" His eyes met hers hopefully, and Willie smiled, winding her arms around his neck and drawing his lips back down to hers.

"Yes," she murmured, finding his lips and covering them with her own. A thought suddenly occurred to her, and she drew back, a frown on her face. "What about T.C.? How is he going to feel about all this?"

"I'll explain it to you later." Ryce bent down and scooped Willie up in his arms. "I love you, Willie," he said again, as if he couldn't quite believe it himself.

"I love you, too." She met his gaze and saw that the sadness and bleakness had fled, replaced by a wonderful shining light.

"I need you, Willie," he whispered huskily, pressing her close and holding on for dear life. "Please, don't ever leave me."

Her heart overflowed as she said the words that would forever bind them together. "I'll never leave you, Michael. *Not ever.*"

"You belong to me, Willie."

"And you belong to me, Michael. I love you," she whispered again, knowing she would never get tired of saying it.

He was loved. He belonged. Ryce smiled as the little space inside of him overflowed with Willie's love.

"Let's go," he said softly, bending to scoop her up in his arms.

"Go? Where are we going?" She would have been perfectly content to stay right here in his arms, forever.

"We're going home, love," he whispered, kissing her softly. "Where we belong, Willie. We're going *home*."

Epilogue

"Willie, honey, are you sleepy?" Ryce asked, his voice shattering the quiet darkness of their bedroom as he tugged on her sheet.

"Yes," she muttered firmly, pulling the sheet out of his grasp to wind it more tightly around her. "You're being rude," she mumbled sleepily, and Ryce laughed.

"But I'm not rough, am I?" he whispered suggestively, gently touching her in ways that never failed to incite and excite her.

"Have you got a minute, Willie?" he whispered against her lips, and Willie's eyes flew open. He tried not to laugh at the look on her face.

"A minute?" she grumbled, playfully slapping his hands away. "What on earth have *you* got in mind that only takes a minute?"

Ryce laughed softly, slowly teasing her with his touch. She sighed deeply as her body began to warm and respond to him. God, would it always be like this, she wondered happily. Would she always want to be with him, near him.

"Willie?" he murmured, dipping his head to nuzzle her ear. His lips teased her, delighting her as they wove a trail of heat and desire across her tender skin. "I was wondering— Well, I've got to ask you something."

She smiled in the darkness. Sometimes he still had trouble verbalizing his thoughts, his feelings, but he was learning.

"I remember what happened the last time you asked me something, Ryce. Remember where that led?" she asked with a chuckle, throwing one bare leg over his.

"Yes," he murmured, planting a bouquet of kisses across her shoulder. "Vividly. But this is something different."

"That's what they all say," she returned, sighing happily as she reacquainted herself with the warmth and hardness of his body.

"I've been thinking, hon. T.C.'s almost thirteen now. Don't you think it's time he had a sister?"

"A sister?" Willie's soft laughter filled their darkened bedroom. "Honey, there're some things even *you* can't control." She reached up and stroked his cheek. "Besides, I thought we decided that I'd keep on working for another year. You've just started your practice, and even though you're an attorney now, it's going to be a while before we can live on just your salary."

"I know," he whispered, coaxing her with his hands, his lips, until she was desperate for him. "But, I was thinking. I ran into this kid at the shelter today.

A little girl, she's about ten and the most ragtag kid you've ever seen. She's got the foulest mouth I've ever heard," he said with a laugh. "She's a cute little thing, or at least she will be when we get her cleaned up."

Willie wound her arms around him, pressing herself firmly against him. "When *we* get her cleaned up?" she whispered, knowing that the matter was already decided, and not minding in the least. Ryce had so much love to give to her, to T.C., to Morty. There was plenty of love left over. "We'll have to move, you know."

"I know," Ryce murmured, dropping hot, moist kisses on her shoulder.

"I guess we'll have to tell Morty to move the sign, too."

Ryce lifted his head and gazed at the sign T.C. had given to Willie last Mother's Day. It hung over their bed. It read, Sherlock's Home. He smiled.

"Yep," Ryce said softly, pulling Willie closer. "I guess we'll have to move it over and find a house where there's plenty of room for more signs."

"'Signs,' plural, Michael? I've only got one sign."

"It's just a beginning, Willie. We've got lots of room in our hearts for more...signs, don't we?" he asked hopefully, and she smiled, her heart full of love.

"Oh, Michael," she whispered. "I love you."

"I love you, Willie." After two years, the words came easily to him now, but he still loved the sound of them.

"I need you, Michael."

"I need you, too, Willie," he said softly, his eyes shining with love and contentment. He was quiet for a long moment.

"Willie?"

"What, Michael?"

"Are you *sure* you're sleepy?"

* * * * *

*Don't miss Sharon De Vita's ITALIAN
KNIGHTS, where Smooth, Suave Sal
Giordiano finds the women of his dreams in his
own backyard. Coming in November from
Silhouette Romance.*

from
Nora Roberts

Skin Deep

Available September 1988

The third in an exciting new series about the lives and
loves of triplet sisters—

In May's *The Last Honest Woman* (SE #451), Abby
finally met a man she could trust... then tried to
deceive him to protect her sons.

In July's *Dance to the Piper* (SE #463), it took some
very fancy footwork to get reserved recording mogul
Reed Valentine dancing to effervescent Maddy's
tune....

In *Skin Deep* (SE #475), find out what kind of heat it
takes to melt the glamorous Chantel's icy heart.
Available in September.

THE O'HURLEYS!

**Join the excitement of
Silhouette Special Editions.**

SSE 475

SET SAIL FOR THE SOUTH SEAS
with
BESTSELLING AUTHOR
EMILIE RICHARDS

This month Silhouette Intimate Moments begins a very special miniseries by a very special author. *Tales of the Pacific*, by Emilie Richards, will take you to Hawaii, New Zealand and Australia and introduce you to a group of men and women you will never forget.

In Book One, FROM GLOWING EMBERS, share laughter and tears with Julianna Mason and Gray Sheridan as they overcome the pain of the past and rekindle the love that had brought them together in marriage ten years ago and now, amidst the destructive force of a tropical storm, drives them once more into an embrace without end.

FROM GLOWING EMBERS (Intimate Moments #249) is available now. And in coming months look for the rest of the series: SMOKESCREEN (November 1988), RAINBOW FIRE (February 1989) and OUT OF THE ASHES (May 1989). They're all coming your way—only in Silhouette Intimate Moments.

IM249-R

COMING NEXT MONTH

#598 VALLEY OF RAINBOWS—Rita Rainville
Liann Murphy respected the mysteries of Hawaii's past while Cody Hunter
understood the promises of its future. Could they build their dream
together in the magical valley of rainbows?

#599 SIMPLY SAM—Deana Brauer
For years Jake Silvercloud had known Samantha Smith as "tagalong"
tomboy Sam, but she'd grown up—with a vengeance—and Sam was ready
to lead the handsome rancher on a merry, loving chase....

#600 TAKING SAVANAH—Pepper Adams
Her former husband, Beau, had knocked Southern belle Savanah Winslow
off her feet with the news that they were still married. Could she resist
giving the brash Yankee another chance?

#601 THE BLAKEMORE TOUCH—Diana Reep
As his public relations consultant, Christina Hayward had to preserve
Marc Blakemore's glittering image—and maintain a professional distance.
But Marc's masterful touch was getting a firm grip on her heart....

#602 HOME AGAIN—Glenda Sands
Nicki Fox's high-school crush on Kenneth Blackwell had meant nothing—
until she went back home and found herself working with him. Now old
feelings were becoming a very adult chemistry....

#603 ANY SUNDAY—Debbie Macomber
Marjorie Majors was never squeamish—unless she got ill. Dr. Sam Bretton
had allayed her fears with his charming bedside manner, and now
Marjorie needed his *loving* care...forever.

AVAILABLE THIS MONTH:

**#592 JUSTIN—Book 2 of the
LONG, TALL TEXANS trilogy**
Diana Palmer

#593 SHERLOCK'S HOME
Sharon De Vita

#594 FINISHING TOUCH
Jane Bierce

#595 THE LADYBUG LADY
Pamela Toth

#596 A NIGHT OF PASSION
Lucy Gordon

**#597 THE KISS OF A
STRANGER**
Brittany Young

ATTRACTIVE, SPACE SAVING BOOK RACK

Display your most prized novels on this handsome and sturdy book rack. The hand-rubbed walnut finish will blend into your library decor with quiet elegance, providing a practical organizer for your favorite hard-or soft-covered books.

Only $9.95

Approximately 16" x 8" when assembled

Assembles in seconds!

To order, rush your name, address and zip code, along with a check or money order for $10.70* ($9.95 plus 75¢ postage and handling) payable to *Silhouette Books*.

Silhouette Books
Book Rack Offer
901 Fuhrmann Blvd.
P.O. Box 1396
Buffalo, NY 14269-1396

Offer not available in Canada.

BKR-2A

*New York and Iowa residents add appropriate sales tax.

Silhouette Romance

LONG, TALL TEXANS

A Trilogy by Diana Palmer

Bestselling Diana Palmer has rustled up three rugged heroes in a trilogy sure to lasso your heart! The titles of the books are your introduction to these unforgettable men:

CALHOUN

In June, meet Calhoun Ballenger. He wants to protect Abby Clark from the world, but can he protect her from himself?

JUSTIN

Calhoun's brother, Justin—the strong, silent type—has a second chance with the woman of his dreams, Shelby Jacobs, in August.

TYLER

October's long, tall Texan is Shelby's virile brother, Tyler, who teaches shy Nell Regan to trust her instincts—especially when they lead her into his arms!

Don't miss CALHOUN, JUSTIN and TYLER—three gripping new stories coming soon from Silhouette Romance!